P9-CBP-434

LADY FORTUNE

Books by Janet Templeton

LADY FORTUNE

THE SCAPEGRACE

LOVER'S KNOT

LADY FORTUNE

JANET TEMPLETON

DOUBLEDAY & COMPANY, INC.
GARDEN CITY, NEW YORK
1984

All of the characters in this book
are fictitious, and any resemblance
to actual persons, living or dead
is purely coincidental.

Library of Congress Cataloging in Publication Data

Templeton, Janet, 1926–
Lady Fortune.
I. Title.
PS3558.E78L3   1984   813'.54
ISBN 0-385-19233-9

Library of Congress Catalog Card Number 83–20543

First Edition

For
Veronica Mixon
with the best of good wishes

LADY FORTUNE

CHAPTER ONE

"Depend on it," said Lady Fairfield, entering the large saloon on the lower floor of her residence, "your daughter will create a difficulty."

"Now why should *our* daughter do anything like that?" Sir Osric asked patiently, having corrected his dear wife's factual omission. "Camilla enjoys a pleasant night out as well as does any young girl."

"Certainly, but not in the company of her elders."

Sir Osric looked over his reading spectacles and allowed himself a sigh. He was used to acting as intermediary between wife and unmarried daughter. He had been made a knight by Queen Vickie because of similar services in a matter of contention among foreign ambassadors. Speaking softly amid domestic strife posed no serious difficulty for him by comparison, but it could be wearing. Opportunities for rest were few and far between.

"She will appear shortly and doubtless be prepared to join us for the revels," said Sir Osric in a tone that could cool the antagonism between shouting diplomats.

"Your very certainty makes me doubtful," said Lady Fairfield, adopting a viewpoint that would never have occurred to a statesman. Determinedly she rang the handbell. "Blackhouse, tell Annie to ask Miss Camilla to join us."

She smiled grimly at her spouse when the butler had embarked on his errand. "You will see, Osric, how well I know that young lady. Camilla won't be formally dressed and will show regret at having to join us for the night."

Sir Osric was inclined to agree that time spent with parents who were distressed about her being unmarried by the ripe age of twenty was not a young girl's idea of bliss. Knowing their daughter, however, he supposed that Camilla would be prepared to make the best of it for a while. He settled back and waited in this high-ceilinged room, with a row of windows open to the April breeze, a wall of bookcases with volumes in two languages, and twin deep chairs and small tables on either side of a dark sofa. With a copy of the latest *Athenaeum* on his lap and the spectacles now deposited on the nearest table, he looked like some scholar taking his ease.

There was a polite knock on the door. Lady Fairfield turned to her husband, wanting him to admit the person who would prove him to have been wrong.

"Enter."

Miss Camilla Fairfield, having obeyed that request, smiled impartially at the just and the unjust alike. She had been favored by the gods, and at twenty still kept the looks of her tenderest years. Under bright blond hair crimped in ringlets across the forehead, she displayed a fair skin, candid blue eyes, a perky nose, and generous lips. It was her own conviction that her chin was too pronounced, but perhaps she had encouraged herself to think so because it was hard otherwise to accept the classic suitability of her remaining features. As for her figure, it was delightful without being what a wag might have considered as unnecessarily obtrusive. Certainly she was a credit to her family.

At the sight of her costume, Sir Osric masked a smile and Lady Fairfield bit her lip to keep from showing consternation because of their daughter's unexpected obedience. Camilla was arrayed in white satin cut high at the waist and low at the corsage. Accenting the whiteness and slim, bare arms was a scarlet sash.

One look at her parents convinced Camilla that her father had won his point in some argument about her. She didn't show pleasure at the knowledge, which might have angered her mother. In character Camilla resembled her considerate male parent, just as in appearance she very much favored the Lady Fairfield of twenty-five years ago.

"You look most attractive," Sir Osric said, eyes twinkling, as his wife hid her confusion with fussy little gestures as though she was physically uncomfortable. "You will be the comeliest girl at the *musicale* in Baron Colquitt's residence."

"Thank you, Father."

Lady Fairfield said irritably, "It will do you little good, Cammie, if you don't search out prospects in the marriage market. Younger girls will be there and doing so."

"Yes, Mamma," Camilla agreed, her face impassive.

"It is more than overdue that you find a young male in society who will offer for you," Lady Fairfield said briskly, still using her complaint to hide her anger at having been proved wrong.

Rather than beginning a quarrel, Camilla lowered her eyes modestly. Had she chosen to speak, she would have reminded Lady Fairfield about Louise, her sister. The older girl had married three years ago, in '40, at the age of eighteen. Her husband, the dashing young Anthony Passy, son of the portrait painter, had turned into a wastrel who had set himself the task of drinking away Louise's dowry. Knowledge of her sister's marital difficulties was enough to prejudice Camilla so that she'd carefully consider a likely candidate for matrimony. Her cautiousness, although perfectly understandable, had driven off more than one impetuous male.

"You won't have your looks much longer," her mamma remarked, as if for the first time, in discussing the future. "I've shown you the sons of Earls and Viscounts, Dukes and Barons, not to mention Scottish peers and Irish peers, a son of the Lord Great Chamberlain of England and a son of the Lord High Commissioner. All with no results. I hardly know who else suitable is left."

Camilla silently drew a breath of relief at hearing that Mamma had exhausted her list of choices, or so it seemed. One of Mamma's habits was to display Camilla to young men who were totally unsuitable for her in terms of temperament, as if proving that Camilla, in desperation, must accept the least desirable of masculine companions. No doubt such measures helped Mamma convince herself that everything possible was being done with a daughter's true interests in mind. For Camilla to raise that issue, however respectfully, would only have stoked fires which were already smoldering, and she had learned some rudiments of diplomacy, at least, from her father.

Her mother continued, "Now that I think of it, however, there is one exception." Having hopefully succeeded in frightening her daughter, it was time to offer the possibility of relief. "A new arrival in London."

Camilla's face didn't lose that modest look, but she was unable to keep from feeling wary. If Mamma wanted to display some young man to her, then that male was almost certainly not worth even the lightest flirtation. In her mind's eye appeared the image of one more blank-faced, snuff-spraying, red-nosed young swell in that series with which Mamma had confronted her as possible husbands.

"Good news is always most welcome," she murmured discreetly.

Father pursed his lips with such quickness that he must have been restraining a smile at such overly pointed tact.

"This is certainly going to be very good news for some girl who has not yet received an offer," Lady Fairfield intoned. "The young man of whom I speak has newly inherited a title. Further, he has ample holdings in Kent, I believe. There is a rent roll and fund money. He is the recipient—if my information is correct—of fully five hundred pounds a year, and has a seat in Parliament as well."

Camilla had heard of some newly titled arrival from one of her numerous friends, and had retained some hope for this stranger as a prospective partner in the dance of life. At Mamma's hymn of praise, however, her heart sank.

"He is a Duke," Mamma added, a note of reverence appearing in her voice. "The Duke of Strafford." She sighed. "I suppose that half a hundred younger females in the City have already set their caps in his direction."

Sir Osric intruded. "I feel sure that Camilla can be the successful one if she chooses to be."

Lady Fairfield ignored her husband's attempt to gain his daughter's further esteem while showing sympathy with her own view. Although he, too, wanted Camilla to plight her troth, he permitted his wife to make all the critical observations. As a result he was, in his daughter's eyes, largely sympathetic. She herself was probably considered a virago by her daughter. It was most unfair!

"Fortunately," she said, raising her voice toward Camilla to keep from turning on Osric, "the Duke will deign to attend tonight's *musicale* at Baron Colquitt's, and you will have one chance, Camilla, to fascinate him."

"I see." Camilla was appalled by Mamma's harsh tone, as if to say that no other opportunity would ever materialize for a desiccated spinster of twenty summers. She had been informed not two days ago by the Colquitt girls that the Duke of Strafford might attend their *musicale*. With her hopes now gone because of Mamma's anxious urging, the Duke's agenda made no difference to her any longer.

"In short, then," Mamma began.

No new matters of fact were to be discussed, so Camilla suggested calmly, "I hope I may be excused to return to my room and further arrange my hair."

She departed as soon as Mamma gave the needed permission. The conversation had imbued her with a great desire to escape from this night's so-called festivities. These would only be an excuse for husband-hunting by a number of young ladies in society or with good friends who were situated that way. It was going to be impossible for her to enjoy the mildest flirtation, and every tilt of the head would have to be adjudged as to whether or not it showed her off most attractively. As for the music which was to be heard, it could be considered nothing less than a needed intrusion. It was the sort of evening from which Camilla would have fled if she had been in control of her own destiny.

On the second level of the house she hesitated. Sounds of stirring could be heard from her brother's room. She wondered if Arthur would be making himself available on this night to the attentions of the demoiselles Colquitt. If not, which seemed more likely, he might be of some aid in this exquisitely sordid dilemma. At the very least he might be prevailed upon to suggest some suitably draconian measure which hadn't yet occurred to her.

She proceeded down the hallway, hardly needing the illumination provided by flickering lights in silver brackets spaced judiciously apart. Arthur's door was the third on the left, and he threw it open as soon as she knocked.

He was two years older than his sister, and sported their mother's fair skin allied, in his case, to Sir Osric's large eyes and thin lips. Women considered him handsome but not the last word in male beauty. Despite clothes like the high collar and cravat he was currently wearing with satin waistcoat and breeches, he wasn't known as a swell. Presumably this was because he hadn't stayed in one place long enough to earn that designation. His idea of a night's pleasure was to attend half a dozen places new to him.

"Come in, do," Arthur said agreeably, welcoming any diversion from solitude.

Camilla spared but one glance at the best room that any of the Fairfield siblings had ever been given under the family roof, enough to reassure her that nothing had been altered and no comment was required about some change. A high-ceilinged room with walls papered in vertical black and orange stripes, and windows with orange plush curtains, it boasted that type of square and durable furniture with which a young man's room could be blessed but never a woman's. Camilla promptly deposited herself on a crocodile chair and began to speak, choosing her words with care.

"You look far too eager and elated for someone who plans to attend a *musicale*," she remarked.

"I wouldn't be found within a million miles of the hideous event," Arthur said blithely. "Besides, Mamma feels strongly that I must not let myself become the target of husband-hunting girls."

Camilla wished fervently that their mother would have said something comparable to her about dealing with males.

Arthur, reminded by those words of his sister's marital state, looked questioningly at her. "And when are we going to have another wedding in the family? It's about time you blighted some young man's life for him."

She answered earnestly, "As soon as I feel certain that my marriage won't repeat the disaster that Louise's marriage has been."

Arthur acknowledged their sister's domestic woes with a taut nod. "That might require a long courtship from a normally impatient male. Difficult situation."

"I am aware of that."

He looked sympathetic, a condition which she saw only too seldom in other members of the family. It tempted her to speak further about her problems.

"And Mamma, as ever, is finding hideous males to offer for me," she added. "Tonight it is planned for some pestiferous Duke to inspect me and presumably count my teeth as well."

"The Duke of Strafford, do you mean? He must be the only peer you don't know, and that ignorance is caused by his having just arrived to take his father's seat in the wax gallery."

She smiled briefly at the mention of that popular name for the House of Lords. "I'm sure that if Mamma considers him a catch he must be horrid."

"I don't remember the fellow, but then I speak to so many in the course of an afternoon. I certainly have been introduced."

"He is probably the one whose face is covered with red spots now that he is approaching boyhood."

"I'm sure he must be up to snuff or I'd recall him vividly."

"Well, he's certainly not memorable or outstanding."

"To a gel he might be," Arthur said reasonably. "How am I to know what sort of fellow would be considered handsome by a gel?"

Camilla didn't chose to remark that if the Duke was at all prepossessing, Mamma was not likely to see him as a possible mate for her. Arthur wouldn't understand such reasoning. As a male and Mamma's favorite among the children, he was treated very differently from Camilla or Louise when the latter had lived in the nest.

"I feel that the evening will be difficult for me," she said, putting her complaint in terms he could understand. "I would like to be elsewhere."

"Not that I blame you, Sister. I myself plan to start the night at Royde's, the new gambling house on Bennet Street off Piccadilly. Just opened, you know. I've told everybody to join me there tonight by ten." He shrugged. "Which doesn't aid you, I fear. No help for it but that you must be a good little girl and go shopping in the marriage market tonight."

She found it painful to hear his best opinion. With his aid or without it, however, her agile brain sought for an effective *modus.*

"Perhaps I can arrange to put in only a very brief appearance at the Colquitt hovel."

He guffawed. "I certainly wish you luck, but you must pardon me if I remain doubtful."

Her opinion corresponded with his, but she held her head higher. "Perhaps we will both be surprised tonight."

She spoke so fervently that he responded with a smile. "I hope so, Sister, if that's what you wish."

"I want to spend a pleasant evening in which I consider anything but marriage," she said sincerely. "But I don't think I shall be able to accomplish that much till I am myself married."

For a moment she didn't understand why her brother chuckled. To her credit, when she did realize the meaning of what she had just said, she joined him.

CHAPTER TWO

The Fairfield carriage, a shiny berlin with two footmen up and a half-asleep coachman guiding glossy bays, left the front of the house at Lower Brook Street. Before long it was moving down New Burlington Street, with its rows of stone hitching posts and curtained windows. By the time the vehicle had been turned left and was proceeding down Savile Row, the three people inside the closed box were beginning to stir restlessly.

Sir Osric, in blue superfine and with a white shirt and thick cravat, pinched-in coat, and black hat, had the drawn and tired look that Camilla would have associated with a man who confronted an errand in diplomacy. Mamma, on the other hand, seemed worried—and was certainly vocal.

"Now Cammie, dear, you must not attempt to be cynical at the Duke's expense," she said, issuing instructions as though Camilla had never before encountered a youthful male in his native habitat. "You must be polite and respectful, but keep him at arm's distance. Yet you must indicate clearly that upon better acquaintance you can be the woman he will worship above all others."

"Yes, Mamma."

She would at that moment have indicated her own tiredness with the subject but remembered Mamma talking in the past about not having met Father until she was at the ripe age of nineteen. Shortly before then Mamma had arrived in the City from Chipping Norton in Oxfordshire, and with no kith or kin but older cousins. The fear of possibly being unmarried and alone in London was one that she had never forgotten, and it spurred her to marry off her female children whether they willed it or not, whether or not they would be happy with the partners chosen for them.

"You must convince him that you sympathize with his aspirations—if, that is, he has any."

"Yes, Mamma," Camilla said, unable to keep from sounding irritable as Lady Fairfield paused for breath.

The latter bridled. "There is no need to take that tone with me," she insisted, effectively destroying such reserves of sympathy as Camilla had been able to muster.

While Lady Fairfield continued to speak along those lines, Camilla glanced at her father. Sir Osric looked sympathetic to her but spoke no word. It never occurred to Camilla to wish that Father would interfere long enough to tell Mamma that continual discussion of the same subject was unlikely to cause a desired effect.

The carriage skittered to a halt at long last, permitting the family to descend. Linkboys were on hand to light the way to that dark red brick double-front house in which the Baron and his Lady had their residence. Men and women had arrayed themselves around the dingy white pillars and were exchanging pleasantries.

Camilla, of course, knew all the younger ones and greeted them. She was considering a flirtation when the double doors to the house opened. The foyer of the Colquitt home was deserted.

"Does no one else have the fiber of character to expose herself to music?" Camilla inquired, not too loudly, and promptly entered.

Her cloak and gloves given to the care of servants, she was able to examine the foyer more closely. It had been newly decorated in the Chinese fashion, with black lacquer wall panels, fringed silk, lamps on low black teakwood tables, and what were fondly considered depictions of scenes in China. The room could have been displayed to good effect in some museum but sowed discomfort as part of a residence.

Baron and Lady Colquitt rushed forward to welcome the

guests who were now seeping into the house. Because the Fairfields had led the flight from pleasure, they were given more time than most of the others.

"How lovely both you females look," said Lady Colquitt with a broad, insincere smile. She wore a bright gown previously soaked in water to show off her billowing figure with some accuracy, a sight which startled other male visitors. Her eyes moved from Lady Fairfield's respectably dark gown with its darker border, to Camilla's white satin with a scarlet sash. "And in feature, my dears, I must say that the two of you seem like sisters."

Lady Fairfield was far too good-mannered to take offense where none was intended. "Thank you, but I have no wish to be considered a sister of my daughter's. I am a settled woman, as must be clear to all."

Lady Fairfield glanced at Camilla, perhaps hoping to see envy in her daughter's eyes. Camilla's face was without expression. Quickly the mother turned away.

"Of course, my dear," Lady Colquitt said hastily.

Mamma changed the subject to one of greater concern. "I don't see the Duke of Strafford among those present."

"Oh, you will know as soon as he arrives, because every young girl in the room will be after him," Lady Colquitt said with a smile of amusement. "My own little pigeons, to be sure, won't be able to participate in the sport, as they will be showing their social accomplishments."

Camilla realized belatedly that the entire function had been staged only to offer the Colquitt girls an opportunity to display their social adeptness to this unknown peer. Impishly she hoped that the Duke of Strafford would be some fifty years old and with all his teeth gone, if only so that Camilla could note the aggrieved astonishment in so many greedy eyes.

At the far end of this foyer was a double door painted in orange, with gold curlicues. These decorations ceased to pain the eyes when the portals were opened onto the drawing room. Mamma hung back with an unwilling Camilla in hopes of observing the entrance of a strange male. In no time, however, they were soon collected and hauled into the net with the others.

The recital began in the drawing room, which now probably held every comfortable chair for miles around, no matter what its style. Musical notes emerged from the recesses of a piano played by Marcy Colquitt, while her sister sang. Camilla formed the impression that Marcy showed some skill at playing a tune.

In front and behind her, auditors shifted impatiently in their seats, having long ago given up looking back of them to the door. The Duke hadn't presented himself, which, for all purposes, left the pagan ritual without a human sacrifice.

Camilla, with Mamma at her left and Father at hers, leaned over and whispered hopefully, "Some are leaving this temple of the arts."

"All the more reason for us to stay," Father whispered in return. "We have to be among those who congratulate the Colquitts on a successful evening and praise the proficiency of their children."

Camilla wasn't surprised that a diplomat would find himself in deep thought along those lines.

There was a pause after the current selection lurched to a halt. Not till the piano music began once more was another opportunity offered for whispering.

Mamma said grimly, "Yes, indeed, we must stay as long as necessary, the way some others will."

Camilla, who had been resigning herself to endure the complete ordeal by melody, raised her head.

"What you want, Mamma, is to wait for the arrival of the Duke of Strafford should he deign to grace what is left of the evening with his presence."

Mamma didn't deny it. "If he arrives after his presence has been despaired of, it would mean your stealing a march on most of the other eligibles, Cammie. Don't forget that."

"It would also mean our convincing all of society that you are desperate to find a husband for me."

Once again Mamma was forthright. "I am indeed desperate."

Camilla looked over at Father, urgently wanting him to intrude with a pacifying remark.

The look was observed by Mamma and its implications noted. "I might add that your father shares my feelings completely, although he contents himself with saying nothing to you of that."

Father didn't deny or agree, merely pursing his lips as if to indicate that he could have spoken volumes if he chose.

Camilla looked rapidly from the discreet parent to the one who was being sufficiently verbal for both of them. She made a decision about her next actions even as she spoke.

"I will proceed home, then send back the carriage, and write a note to the Colquitt girls tomorrow morning," she said firmly.

"You must stay!"

A reason for her unwavering choice had to be given, Camilla realized belatedly, in preference an untrue one. "Most unfortunately, I am indisposed."

"Given these circumstances, it is difficult to believe you."

Camilla didn't suggest, as she was sorely tempted to do, that she recite symptoms to lend conviction to her claim. She hoped, however, that her strained look suggested illness.

As she began to rise, Mamma's hand reached out to keep her in place.

Sir Osric, watching two of his female relatives in a display of temperament, sensed that his wife's voice might be raised within moments, so angry was she.

Quietly he said, "I feel that Camilla's claim should be accepted."

"You know, too, that she is pretending," Lady Fairfield snapped, her voice already hovering dangerously close to an upper register.

"I do not say yes or no to that. What I wish to prevent at this time is a louder discussion."

Lady Fairfield, discerning the wisdom of that observation, raised her hand to free Camilla. Without another word, Camilla rose and started out, tracked remorselessly by the music and singing of her friends.

She recovered her scarlet-lined cloak with its pink hood, which was kind to her eyes, and the reticule as well. The family carriage waited with the others. So pleased was she at the prospect of escape that she didn't follow her usual practice in a vehicle and look back to where she had come from. Otherwise she would have seen a modish deep barouche stop at the curb on Savile Street and a young man emerge before the home of Baron and Lady Colquitt. The young man twitched his shoulders in a gesture that was somewhere between a shrug and a shudder and then hurried inside.

The family carriage threaded its way back to Lower Brook Street. Camilla disembarked and watched it turn to go back to the Colquitt domain.

On the point of entering her home she stopped herself. A passing watchman had called out the hour, and it was far earlier than she had expected. It was only ten o'clock.

Convinced that she had gained at least two unexpected hours, time having passed so slowly in the lair of music, she wanted to compensate herself for that tense period by joining her brother at Bennet Street and watch him joyously throwing away a little of the family monies. She didn't often disport herself in such a fashion, but it sounded amusing on this particular night. Certainly her elders would not arrive back home before twelve, and after a stodgy time the notion of taking an expedition on impulse alone was delightful to her.

Cabs were plentiful, many of them carrying drunkards back to their residences for such rewards as might be obtained from grateful families. One cabbie halted for her, a merry-eyed middle-aged man in a partly crushed topper and with a varicolored shawl around his neck.

"Do you know Royde's gambling house on Bennet Street? Good. Please take me there."

Camilla's cab took her past Piccadilly and down St. James's Street, where the Horse Guards were stationed. The first street on her right as the cab turned was Bennet itself, a short and narrow thoroughfare with respectable-looking houses set closer together than would have been her own preference.

An organ-grinder was cranking out some dolorous tune as Camilla paid the cabman his two and six from her reticule. She walked past the so-called orderly, who was stationed so as to be ready to alarm the porter at first sight of any constables or thief-takers.

In a small and sparsely furnished anteroom an usher divested Camilla of her outer garments, declining to accept her reticule by saying that there was a house directive against doing so. She hoped it wouldn't cause her to feel conspicuous, and then recalled her usual habit before entering gambling rooms.

"One more thing: Do you have a mask? I would rather not be pointed out by anyone."

"Yes, Miss, we always keep a few in stock for such ladies as might wish not to be known." The usher was cadaverous in appearance and looked as if he had escaped the resurrectionists by seconds. "Here you are, Miss."

She chose a mask in azure, it being the color that was most likely to complement her sea blue eyes and soften what she considered a jutting chin. She knew perfectly well that Arthur would recognize her but didn't want to aid anyone else in doing so. No one would see her here again for a long period. Half an hour from now she would be returning to Lower Brook Street so that she would be certain to arrive home before her distinguished progenitors.

A flight of stairs took her to a half-open door and the heart of these premises. They were no larger than others she had seen, where she'd done only enough wagering so as not to be thought negligent in her duties to the goddess of chance. Waiters rushed back and forth carrying trays of food and drink to players so absorbed that they hardly cared for nourishment by the time it arrived. Smoke-thickened voices could be heard advising players to lay their wagers and, soon afterwards, saying that the game was finished and that it was time to lay wagers again.

In only a few moments Camilla realized that Arthur wasn't

gracing the establishment by his presence. Most likely he had come and met some of his friends, as originally planned, then wagered briefly and permitted his restlessness to take him elsewhere. She hid disappointment by telling herself critically that a marriage would cause him to calm down and would be advantageous for Arthur in many ways—as it seemed for most males, to judge by even her limited experience.

"You there!" A man at her elbow called out. She turned to see a red-faced gentleman with a matching nose and a tankard before him. His well-fitting clothes were fashionable and his queue slightly out of the place that artifice had intended. "Would you like to join me?"

She had been turning to leave, but staying at his side briefly would keep this intemperate gamesman from making some loud remark about her and possibly attracting attention. Already she had recognized Bobby Herbert, someday to be the Earl of Pembroke, and the Count of Bessborough was at another table. She didn't want to gain their attention, even if she was withdrawing.

"For a while only," she said, and approached. This table was in the mode, some eighteen feet of surface covered in green baize and rounded at the ends. The large red triangle in the center proved that it had been designed for games of *rouge et noir.* Plainly it wasn't being put to that use now. A pair of dice stood in the center of the table, and at sight of them she looked up.

"Is this a new game?" She was curious.

"It's been put in at my request," the man exulted. "I understand it's all the crack up at Almack's and at Crockford's too."

He spoke with envy, like a man who hadn't been invited to lose money at those temples of recklessness but could afford to have similar conditions reproduced elsewhere for his benefit.

"It's called hazard and depends on the way the dice will fall," he said, gathering his faculties for an explanation. "To start a game, somebody throws the dice. If the upper faces of both show dots amounting to a total of any number from four through ten, that number becomes the one that the player wagers he can repeat. He throws the dice in hopes of doing so, but if he throws a seven he loses his bet and control of the dice as well. Is that clear?"

"Perfectly, thank you."

His next request stopped her from walking off. "Will you wager?"

She didn't want to decline, as he might become drunkenly shrill at the prospect of disappointment.

"Just once," he said, sensing her reluctance. "Just so I can feel I'm truly in a game."

She glanced questioningly at the two players who stood silently nearby, neither dressed to the very height of fashion and looking irritable, as if they had been born with one set of feelings.

"These two are nothing more than puffs," the red-faced man said with a careless wave of a hand which had been roughened years ago by manual work. "They're hired by the bank to make this area look busy and bring in actual players. I can always recognize puffs, so nothing they do makes any matter to me." He added, "Please wager."

She felt sorry for this parvenu, who was pained because he wasn't permitted to better himself socially.

"Only a small amount, you understand."

"Better than nothing, m'dear, and, as I say, I promise not to ask more than once."

From her reticule Camilla drew out a gold sovereign and set it down next to her on the table. The puffs looked sad.

"Ha! I'll drop ten pounds beside your sovereign." Suiting his action to his word, he reached for the dice. These he warmed in both hands, whispering as if to encourage the lifeless bones to victory. He threw a four and followed it by an eight, a five, a ten, a six, a nine, and another five.

At that moment some newly arrived gamesmen came negligently into the room. At a gesture from the table captain one of the puffs moved forward to lay a five-pound note on the table by way of convincing the newcomers that the stakes were higher than was actually the case. That movement jiggled the player's hand, causing the dice to fall before he was ready to let them go. They came down on a total of seven dots, losing the player his bid.

"Game is over," said the table captain as he raked in all the money with a wooden stick forked at a right angle at the far end. As was only to be expected, all bets had been made against the bank.

To this finale the red-faced player took offense. He threw his head back angrily and snapped, "A puff of yours bounced into me as I was making my throw!"

"I'm sorry, sir, but the rules of the bank are clear that a completed throw—"

"Rules be blowed! I've been gammoned!"

At this last remark he raised his voice so loudly that Camilla took three steps back, not wanting to be seen near the man. Before she could proceed to the exit, she realized how much she had underestimated the quickness of various persons engaged at gaming. They were standing now, many attempting to draw closer to the red-faced man in hopes of hearing more details. A continuous murmur could be made out of questions being asked and answered inadequately before being asked of others.

Unable to move farther off, Camilla turned back rather than facing others so closely that they might recognize her in the future at some social occasion.

The man shouted, "This place is a bam, so all of you beware!"

Half a dozen members of the crowd were suddenly parted by a forceful and darkly intense man in his twenties. He wore a long brown surtout with a high velvet collar and frogged buttonholes, all over trousers, and short boots. It was possible to believe, as rumor had it about the late Mr. Brummell, that this one had his boots cleaned in champagne. But any aura of vocational indolence was belied by his busy manner as he moved.

"Now what's all this?" he began quietly, like some thieftaker arrived at the scene of a transgression. "If you have any complaints here, you can always talk to Will Royde first. I'll do fairly by you."

The captain put in, " 'E done 'is throw and says as Ernie bounced 'im."

Royde considered. "The luck must have been against you in the first place, sir, or it wouldn't have happened—certainly it wasn't done on purpose, not at Royde's—and you'd have made your point."

"But that's not fair!"

"Luck isn't fair." Royde looked censorious, his thick brows drawn and lips pressed together. "You make a bet that you'll win and if you don't, then your luck has spoken."

"All I want is simple justice!"

"You are still trying to refuse an obligation to pay because your luck was bad," Royde said sharply. "Till you understand the nature of gaming, sir, you should take your custom elsewhere."

"No, damme! I won't leave till I get what's coming to me."

The captain and both puffs were already moving behind the red-faced man, probably to grant his wish in an unpleasant manner. Camilla realized that there would be further shouting, and the gamesman's resistance would probably earn him a thrashing.

Almost without being aware that she did it, Camilla swiftly looked around and saw no sign of the familiar faces she had noticed here. Perhaps the other players had left between her first observing them on the premises from behind her mask and the start of the red-faced man's gaming with her.

"Just a moment!" she called out, surprised at her own temerity even as she spoke. Several witnesses stepped aside to offer her their space, and the sight of that was enough to give Camilla added confidence that her father's daughter would speak to the best effect.

"Though I was gaming against you and wagered a sovereign," she said clearly to the red-faced man in such tones as to be heard by everyone else in the room, "as you feel so badly about your loss, I will be glad to make it up to you in part by dividing all my night's winnings with you afterwards."

There was a moment's silence and then the room itself seemed to explode with laughter, one gamesman nudging another in the ribs by way of appreciating the masked young lady's humorous offer. The red-faced man, deprived of his chance to seem heroic in a matter of principle, saw that he had become a laughingstock. He seemed to deflate within his clothes. Having shrugged at another lesson in fate's caprices, he started dispiritedly to the door. Probably he remained unaware that the young lady's words had saved him from a severe reckoning with Royde's angered minions.

Royde himself had absorbed the lesson that it was folly to lecture an errant player about the philosophy of his chosen sport when more diplomatic means lay instantly to hand for gaining an objective. He looked intently at his masked pedagogue and smilingly presented himself before her.

"You must permit me to thank you for having intervened so opportunely," he said.

Camilla was aware that he had been impressed by her. The softened voice and intense look into her sea blue eyes gave ample evidence of that. His air of coiled tension caused her to form the thought that he might misunderstand the mildest pleasantry and take her lightly spoken words to be meaningful. It was best to be courteous as ever, but not show any awareness of his feelings or respond to them.

"I was pleased," she murmured, "to assist another player."

It was a distinction that any member of society would have instantly comprehended and probably rewarded with a rueful smile. This humorless man, with his rigid grenadier posture, only made a brusque movement of one hand, as if he had been interrupted in mid-speech.

"You have been most helpful to me, as my establishment here is newly opened. I can assure you that you and yours will be welcome, and I hope to see you often. I can certainly arrange another game in which you might participate now if you wish."

"Thank you, but that won't be necessary."

Royde blinked in surprise. He was a man who was apparently used to drawing entirely favorable responses from females.

To somebody else Camilla would have added that her departure was imminent, but it seemed wisest to communicate as little as possible with this man.

Someone cleared his throat behind her, and Camilla turned to see a player with whom she was slightly acquainted and hadn't recognized in the last moments. He was a blank-faced young swell named Caleb Selwyn, and was known for some mysterious reason as "Egypt Caleb." He was holding out several cards face down.

"Here now, you seem to have been lucky at gaming to-night," said Egypt Caleb, chuckling. He had apparently imbibed too much to recognize Camilla behind the mask. "Would you like to grace my cards and touch 'em for luck?"

It was no less than might have been expected from a swell's mocking humor. She decided that it would be quickest to agree.

A number of others at the gaming tables had looked up. Camilla was asked to do the same for yet another player. She supposed that if anyone did by some chance recognize her, it would be a man who didn't know her well and she could always proffer emphatic denials. Meanwhile, it would be most politic to oblige quickly, not allowing anyone a long look into her masked face. Camilla was amused at herself for not touching the cards of rivals at the gaming table, almost as if she did consider that she had become a living icon of good fortune.

Moving quickly, she observed that the waiters, scurrying with refreshments, showed sufficient agility so as to avoid her path. Royde's expressionless eyes followed her. By this she was just as well pleased, thinking it best to show unmistakably that she felt no interest in paying him the least attention.

The door opened suddenly, causing the sash of her dress to lightly sway. Four men were coming in. Camilla's eyes were riveted on the first of these.

This first among equals was indeed handsome, with regular features and a white skin graced by only the slightest touch of the sun. His nile green eyes glinted even in the artificial light. His body was in good condition, having been used as more than a vehicle for such evening clothes as the white waistcoat, black silk trousers, and dark stockings that he currently sported. The garments and decorations looked as if they had taken shape only moments ago.

He was immersed in talk with another of the men. "I could hardly wait to leave, 'pon my word," he was saying, probably in answer to some question. His tones were intriguingly different from the slurred London accent with which Camilla was so familiar.

"Can't blame you at all," the other said in a Londoner's tones. "Been through it m'self, damme, yes I have! You've just had a difficult night."

"One smiling female after another," the handsome one said, shuddering as he and the others settled into the chairs surrounding a green baize-covered card table while the establishment's banker passed a deck of fresh cards to him. "Heaven knows, I have no scorn for the opposite sex as such, but to see vast shoals of them coming at me, each guided by a mother, is so appalling as to have made the late Casanova himself turn and run. The only thing that any of them has in mind is marriage. None has any thought as to whether I would suit her or if she would make me happy. To these London ladies I am nothing more than meat on a hook."

Camilla could sympathize with a point of view that closely resembled her own. She felt so strongly about it that she found herself moving towards their table, wanting to express her feelings.

One of the young men looked up and saw her approaching. "We have enough players here," he said quietly.

A witness to the écarté play at a nearby table suddenly leaned over and whispered into that man's ear. Presumably he was saying that the masked young woman could touch players' cards and confer luck upon them. As several of those who had been favored by Camilla's touch on their cards had already won, the recommendation must have been impressive. That player looked up smilingly at her, as did two others.

Only the young man whose grievances had caught Camilla's interest, and with whom she wanted to express her agreement, didn't look up. He was busily drawing a card that would help determine which of the others was going to be his partner. The three remaining players followed. His partner was a big-nosed man who chuckled and rubbed his hands at good fortune, no doubt because the handsome one was a skillful gamesman. With hawklike attention he watched the banker pass the deck clockwise for each player to cut and shuffle. By the time he had finished dealing each card face down in rotation, the last could be turned up to show the heart suit. Hearts had become trumps.

Camilla, for some reason she didn't understand, put a palm to her own heart.

"Wait a moment," said the big-nosed man, having observed her action from the corner of his eye. "It's time for the masked girl to give us luck."

She touched the big-nosed man's cards from the back. The handsome one absently went along with the ritual, in which he didn't believe, holding up his cards. Camilla touched these gingerly with two fingers only, so that it took a little more time to make the circuit, and her fingers almost touched his strong yet graceful ones. She didn't trust herself to look into his eyes and continue her part in this newly evolved ritual.

As soon as she drew back the game began. The men settled themselves to discover whose skills would bring forth the first victory. Camilla watched the handsome one give himself over to this activity, using every fiber of his will. It was difficult for her to look elsewhere.

Her sense of hearing, however, could not be centered on the game. From outside a watchman clearly called the hour. She realized with sinking feelings that she had to leave immediately if she didn't want to possibly rouse her elders' ire.

She gave a last regretful look at the handsome young man. He was almost bereft of cards by now. As she turned, he suddenly spoke a little more loudly than before, and in the slightly unusual mode of speech she had previously noted.

"Our trick, partner!"

It pleased Camilla to know that he had won.

The big-nosed player apparently looked up and said unhappily, "Why, the girl is going before we can even thank her."

Camilla recognized the opportunity for that flirtatious byplay she craved, perhaps leading to other meetings with the handsome one. But she could not possibly take advantage of it at this particular time.

The handsome man said wryly, "If Lady Fortune slips away, we're dished for the rest of the night."

Camilla happened to catch one last glimpse of Will Royde's angry features, his eyes moving from her to the whist players and back. Then she rushed out. Until she had reclaimed her belongings and given back the mask, she wasn't certain that she'd be able to resist the temptation of going back. She wanted to walk slowly at least and savor the recollection of these last moments while still on the premises, but she was a prisoner of time and could not do so.

On Bennet Street she searched anxiously for a cab, aided by the torches of linkboys trudging mournfully back and forth. The driver of the third oncoming cab turned out to be a cheery gent who agreed to return Camilla without delay to Lower Brook Street and home.

She settled down in the musty cab and reflected upon the last half hour of this difficult night. Certainly it had been absorbing and she was delighted by the pseudonym of Lady Fortune. Uppermost in her mind, though, was the consideration as to whether or not she would ever see that very handsome man again.

Not under any circumstances would she prefer to visit Royde's again in hopes of making another contact with him; the difficult and disconcerting presence of Royde himself would keep her from any action along those lines. As for the handsome one, he was sufficiently wealthy to tempt the gods by gaming, but such largesse didn't assure him a place as a swaggering swell. If he mattered at all in society, however, their paths must cross yet again.

That thought should have been calming, but hardly had her cab reached Piccadilly when she was struck by a conception so plain that she wondered why it hadn't come to her a while ago. She supposed she had been too shaken at seeing a most handsome man with whose views she had much in common, but she was surprised all the same by her flawed understanding.

The young man had been subjected earlier this night to an onslaught of husband-hunting females. Therefore he was almost certainly the same one she had been dragooned into seeing on this night, and one of those whom he had escaped. The self-assured young man must be none other than the Duke of Strafford, upon whom Mamma had hoped to wish her off.

For once Mamma had chosen interestingly. It was Lady Fortune who had unwittingly betrayed her own best interests.

CHAPTER THREE

It was a subdued Camilla who entered the morning room on Lower Brook Street at eight o'clock. Early May sunlight streamed through the window despite drawn yellow velvet curtains. Lady Fairfield, already in place at the circular table heaped with toast and black tea, took it upon herself to cause her daughter regret for having abandoned the field of honor at the Colquitt *musicale.*

"Such a handsome young man," Lady Fairfield gushed as fried eggs were brought in by the invaluable Blackhouse. "So distinguished, so—not to put too fine a point upon it, Cammie —so infernally handsome."

Camilla winced inwardly but showed interest in nothing but the viands that were available. Her portion of lean bacon was, as usual, small. Mamma claimed that bacon exercised a ghastly effect upon the figure. Never did Mamma forget to add, though, that when Camilla became mistress of her own ménage she would, of course, be able to billow out as she chose. Mamma's idea of enticing a girl into wedlock apparently consisted of claiming that it was proper that a girl spend her early years attracting a male and could therefore spend her married years repelling him. It was not a point of view that was likely to win a young girl's sympathy, but of this consideration Lady Fairfield was entirely unaware.

"I'm sure he was inspected by all the ladies, this Duke of yours," Camilla said, recollecting Strafford's disdain of them *en masse,* as shown at Royde's gambling hell on the preceding night. "Perhaps he is occupied this morning in choosing one of the damsels to offer for, picking the winning name out of slips of paper previously lodged in his best beaver hat."

"I never saw a more handsome man," Mamma said sternly, not letting herself be distracted by frivolous interpolations from an erring daughter. "Godlike, I tell you, with eyes as green as grass swaying in a field."

In Camilla's view the Duke's eyes had seemed more like the green of seawater, a nile green. Mamma's having remarked upon them, however, as Camilla herself had silently done, set the seal upon her conviction that the young gamesman she had observed last night was indeed Strafford himself and not some other exasperated male in full flight from the marriageable daughters of London society.

"What matters, Cammie, is that you should have seen the Duke and that he should have seen you," Lady Fairfield insisted. "Indeed, it was remiss of you not to make yourself available. Your father would agree with me if he could have brought himself to be present this morning."

Camilla felt that Mamma's tone made it entirely understandable that Sir Osric had decided to spend the morning elsewhere and thereby avoid such lively discussion as was bound to ensue over his morning hot chocolate. It never occurred to Camilla that her father's services as a peacemaker would have been most welcome at the table.

"Your brother, too, would be in agreement with my views," Mamma added, pursuing the quarry to yet another position. "Many a time and often Arthur has said to me that you should be married, and that time cannot be spared to attain that worthy goal."

Camilla doubted if Arthur had considered her situation at all except in conversation with his remaining unmarried sister. Camilla felt sure that Arthur was now in his bed in the best room in the house, sleeping away the effects of his previous night's dissipations. Mamma never urged Arthur to the breakfast table or made him uncomfortable when he did choose to manifest himself.

"I do not know that the Duke would be interested in any one girl amidst shoals of them," Camilla said quickly. An indication that her mind was not closed in this matter would have the effect, as she hoped, of quieting her immediate maternal ancestor. It was unnecessary to remark that some interest had been awakened in her by Strafford's handsome appearance at William Royde's gambling house. "I will perhaps see him again. Society moves in small circles."

"So you now regret your previous inaction," Mamma said, satisfied. A challenge having been indirectly offered, however, she rose to it. "He must see you at a time when fewer of the young women are available for immediate inspection and perhaps for unfortunate comparisons."

Camilla had started to nod, but at the indication that younger females would *per se* be more desirable, she briefly reverted to sarcasm.

"I might make a speech in the Lords."

Mamma, of course, took it seriously. "Not even Queen Victoria could accomplish that in this year of 1843. Have no fear, however, Cammie. I will give the matter my best reckoning."

Mamma obviously meant to be of aid.

Camilla inclined her head appreciatively, although her expectations were slight. Secluding a potentially marriageable young male was probably beyond the powers of any but the Queen and her Teutonic Prince Consort.

"And now," Mamma said, having concluded the repast long after her daughter, "go upstairs and put on your best mantle and poke-bonnet. A day's shopping lies ahead of us, and I will want to see some new dresses for you. After all, you are beginning to show some interest in your position in life at long last, and you should be suitably costumed for this blessed development."

After such a reaction, Camilla found herself thinking rebelliously that it was not always pleasurable in this life to have wholehearted allies.

Lady Fairfield's efforts to tree the elusive Duke proved fruitless. Strafford seemed always en route to Parliament or returning to his home in Kent. It was known to her that he kept rooms in the Albany on the north side of Piccadilly but was never observed to be in residence.

Sir Osric, with his university background, made an apt comparison when he was first apprised of these facts.

"It would seem that the young man's oak is sported," he said, the corners of his lips twitching.

"I am not aware of the meaning of that term, nor can I imagine that you would be humorous about such a matter, but I do know that Strafford is most inconsiderate. Most!"

"Quite so, my dear," the diplomat said, promising his aid belatedly in seeking out the young man.

Lady Fairfield correctly guessed that he would move with reluctance in disturbing another male, even if it meant possibly marrying off an aging daughter. In this her suspicions proved correct. Sir Osric either forgot to make contact with the young man when that was possible or said that the Duke was far too occupied with some undoubtedly trivial matter in the Lords.

In this position the matter stood on the night of the May Ball, given, as was their yearly custom, by the Viscount Yeltoun and his amiable Viscountess. It was an occasion which Camilla could hardly refuse to grace with her presence. She had been reliably informed that Arthur, her scamp of a brother, would forego the drink and the gambling long enough to join his family.

The Fairfields arrived in their carriage, with two up, early in the evening. Annie, the maid who had been in the service of the Fairfields since Osric's gilded youth, joined them to minister to those females who might later need help in cosmetic matters. Her proximity was additional evidence that the May Ball was regarded as a social occasion of importance.

For an experienced guest like Lady Fairfield, it was as nothing to sneer silently at the dark red turkey carpet under her feet, look away from the polished mahogany tables, shield her eyes as if the lamps, in their fluted red glass shades, gave far too much light; and then compliment her hostess fulsomely on the excellence of the anteroom's interior. Camilla, watching this performance, doubted if she was ever going to attain

Mamma's level of hypocrisy, nor did she feel that it was a goal toward which she ought to strive.

The Fairfields ascended the stairway up to the ballroom, Mamma not neglecting to say pointedly, if quietly, that the host and hostess were required by manners to be in the ballroom itself and not by the stairs, like so many servants.

"I hope that you, Cammie, are not mistaken for a servant," she added.

Camilla smiled with difficulty. Daughter and mother had quarrelled bitterly about material for the new rose gown purchased from the recently reopened draper's shop of Swan & Edgar's off Regent Street. Mamma detested the necessary armoring of petticoats despite the current mode. As for gaining approval to wear her bright blond hair with a center part, such as the Queen herself now favored, it could have been no more difficult for Hercules to vanquish the Stymphalian birds. A statement that Cammie looked at least moderately well in the current approved fashion (horrendous though it was) had been evolved and issued only after much maternal agonizing.

Camilla ignored Lady Fairfield's pronunciamento any further and looked about her. Truly, it seemed as if most of *le monde* was at hand in this white-walled glossy-floored ballroom. Mothers and daughters surveyed young males as they reached the upper landing, mothers keeping their eyes in that direction even while they spoke to friends who were doing the same. A polka was currently being danced, as pleasant a sight as Camilla had seen for a time. Most likely she would shortly be among those revelers. She was a popular girl, and her expectation was reasonable.

To her son Lady Fairfield said, "You have always been blessedly fastidious in dealing with young ladies. I trust that you will continue to be so."

"Of course, Mamma."

To her daughter, however, Lady Fairfield said sharply, "Turn and face the entrance so that a newcomer may see you among the first. Smile and be vivacious, Cammie. That is what will attract a gentleman."

Camilla nodded, waiting for the first young man to ask

Mamma's permission for a dance and thereby remove her, if only briefly, from parental scrutiny.

Mamma added with some petulance, "Your trouble, Cammie, is that you are always in motion and dancing, but never where more than one young man at a time is able to see you."

Turning away to keep from a new quarrel about the sense of that observation, Camilla was suddenly very still. Standing near the long mahogany table, refreshing himself with a fire-colored liquid in a moderate-sized glass, was the Duke of Strafford himself.

Her first thought was that not even the elusive Duke was able to circumnavigate all obligations of a social nature. Only then did she realize how well he looked. The blue frock coat and white trousers showed his slimness. The white shirt, with its pointed collar turned down over the loosely knotted black tie, was a clear indication that his chest was ample. Camilla suddenly yearned to rest her head upon it.

To her bemused senses no one else was attending the May Ball. She was startled when "Squashed Tom" Curtis asked Mamma to approve his dancing with her. Fiercely she gestured that she wouldn't accept. Mamma acceded to that wish, her features lined by reluctance.

Before Lady Fairfield could question Camilla about such recherché behavior, Camilla's father spoke distractingly to her. Mamma's response was conditioned by the company in which she found herself under this roof, and a need to publicly maintain a facade of serene contentment.

A minor drama was unfolding at this moment within Camilla's sight. One of the older women was approaching the Duke, daughter in tow, a simper on her features. The Duke, startled, widened his magnificent nile green eyes—Mamma's description notwithstanding—and suddenly moved away.

An opportunity, as Camilla shrewdly realized, was about to become available.

It was impossible to know which direction the hunted Duke would take. Camilla felt, though, that in a similar wax she would find someone else with whom to speak, utilizing almost any pretense. Already Strafford was moving in the general direction of a cluster of men who were deep in converse. No doubt he felt that among those worthies he would discover some recent acquaintance with whom to immerse himself in a discussion of matters of importance to gentlemen.

To put herself between the Duke and those preoccupied men was for Camilla the work of a few moments.

Her reward was not long in coming. As she stood smiling vivaciously, much as Mamma had needlessly instructed, she saw out of the corner of her eye that he was drawing closer. At precisely the correct moment she took a step backwards.

At this juncture the Duke cannoned into her. Camilla was briefly off balance but became immediately aware of a firm hand holding her at the waist, steadying her. She now had occasion to regret the new fashion, with its ample petticoats and sturdy horsehair immediately under a soft evening gown.

The Duke, aware of his *faux pas,* stepped back and accordingly withdrew his arm. Camilla seemed to waver. He moved no closer but quickly took both her hands in his, which were dry, warm, and strong.

"I do earnestly beg your pardon, miss," the Duke said in his pleasing baritone. "I am your most humble and obedient."

She decided that it was proper to begin her official relationship to the Duke with a touch of coolness.

"Sir, you have the advantage of me."

Trevor Drawhill, the Duke of Strafford, withdrew his hands as a consequence of her crispness, a regrettable necessity in Camilla's view and his. The Duke looked uncomfortable at having been clumsy in the presence of an attractive and undemanding member of the gentle sex. Nor was he above feeling a moment's gratitude that the girl, and some predatory mother, refrained from hurling themselves upon him.

"I do beg your pardon." His cheeks were coloring slightly. "I was—I was—"

Camilla's sympathy was won by that hesitation. It would be proper, she thought, to test him. A man without some humor congenial to hers would be somebody she could never think of facing on even the most distant of social terms.

She raised her head to minimize the appearance of the chin,

which she always felt was too prominent. A generous smile lit her fine features.

"Would it be correct to say that you were fleeing?"

His forehead darkened further, and Camilla felt that she had presumed too greatly on an acquaintance of such brief duration. The color subsided in a moment, and his lips were puckered at the corners. She felt herself becoming more at ease now.

"I would not myself put it that baldly."

"What would you say, then, in more hirsute terms?"

"I prefer to state that I was withdrawing to a more strategic position, or perhaps that I was consolidating my defenses."

When he smiled Camilla saw for the first time that the gleam in his eyes was physically caused by the irises being a darker green than the nile green of his pupils. This feature of his personage, too, met with her distinct approval.

It was understood that they were friendly, but he had not yet asked her to sport a toe upon the dance floor. Gaining the invitation and accepting it in turn could now be considered by her as suitable goals.

To this end she glanced in that direction. Accommodatingly, and perhaps with gratitude and relief, the Duke cleared his throat.

At this juncture a good-looking maiden and her hesitant mother approached. The girl was only eighteen, with blazing red hair and the clearest skin that another female could but envy. Beatrice Hagthorpe, known to society as "Mad Beatrice," was an aggressive young female not above intruding where she may not have been wanted. Mrs. Hagthorpe, having been prompted by her daughter, smiled with more hesitation than her spawn would surely have preferred.

"A thousand pardons, Your Grace," Mrs. Hagthorpe began awkwardly, "but I had understood that you and my Beatrice were engaged for this dance."

Perhaps it was only the word "engaged" which caused the Duke to recoil from what might otherwise have appeared so delightful a prospect.

Camilla intervened promptly, addressing herself to Mad

Beatrice. "His Grace is promised to me for the remaining dances of the evening."

The Duke nodded swiftly, accepting this stroke of good fortune.

"And now I am fully confident," Camilla said with a smile for the younger female, "that you will pardon us."

As she led the way to the dance floor it was possible to hear Beatrice complaining to her mother about this turn of events, berating the older woman for not having been more forceful on a daughter's behalf.

Waltzes were being danced at this time, the polka music having subsided. The Duke waltzed splendidly, which was suitable. They spoke hardly at all at first, Camilla drawing pleasure from his closeness and the Duke relieved by a narrow escape from the forces of silken commitment.

After a quadrille, with its *pastourelle* and *pantalon* figures, in both of which the Duke handled himself magnificently, Camilla saw that his enjoyment had increased though it remained slightly tentative.

She soothed him by saying, "Beatrice has at last fixed upon another and she and her mamma are lavishing their attentions upon him."

It occurred to her that Trevor, whose full name had been vouchsafed, as had hers, might now choose to make a departure. His objective had been gained and he no longer felt that he was being pursued by some sharp-eyed unmarried female.

Indeed, at the conclusion of the dance he apparently confirmed that suspicion by gesturing her away from the floor. "I have not felt so at ease with a young woman in many months," he said, thereby pleasing her. "I now feel free enough to leave the floor and make peace with your parents."

Once at her mother's side, he suited the action to the word. Lady Fairfield was delighted by her daughter's apparent conquest and cheerfully gave the Duke permission to spend further time in Camilla's company. Sir Osric smiled and nodded, content to shake Trevor's hand while making some meaningless remark in greeting. Of Arthur there was no perceptible sign.

The dance floor was crowded, causing Camilla to wonder if the rose gown could withstand the nearness of so many other revelers. Trevor, looking from her to the crowd and back, seemed to understand her reserve and the reason for it. He gestured toward the nearest balcony. Only some half a dozen couples could be seen under the quarter-moon in the bracing night air.

"One of those other girls, at least, is probably suggesting to her swain that it is a fine night upon which to be married," Trevor said quietly as they took a corner to themselves, his tones rueful.

"In the eyes of many a woman," Camilla felt bound to remark, "finding a husband precludes any other consideration."

"Since coming up from London to take my late father's seat in the Lords, I have been exposed to only that one need on the part of nearly all the respectable young women."

"Are there no girls in Kent who are involved in the hot pursuit of eligible males?"

"Certainly, but those girls seem not to be so intent in the matter." The Duke considered, not wanting to answer carelessly. "At home it is possible to speak with a young lady about hunting or farming and to elicit intelligent and pertinent responses. In London I have found only one civilized and detached young woman, Miss Fairfield, and you are she."

Camilla was pleased at being accepted by this unusual peer with whom she shared a detestation of the humdrum marital chase. In his company, as one result, she felt unaware of any urgent need to draw a proposal of matrimony.

It had crossed her mind earlier that he might be so unusually honest because he recalled their meeting weeks ago in a colorful setting. At that time she had been behind a mask and at William Royde's gambling emporium. In entertaining such a conjecture, however, she was apparently mistaken. He could have seen only her blond hair as set in a different style, and had almost certainly felt too harried to look closely at yet another female.

She found herself speaking to him, in turn, with sincerity. "I don't appreciate having to make myself attractive to a man for the simple reason that he *is* a man. Future happiness cannot result from such a proceeding."

" 'Pon my word it cannot," Trevor agreed. "If affection grows between two people, it would be all very well, but there can be no benefit in forcing it or deluding oneself that one feels anything but congenial."

They beamed in complete agreement, a handsome man and an attractive young woman who could maintain a friendship without keeping an eye out for possible consequences. Camilla couldn't remember when such a feeling of peacefulness had ruled her. As for Trevor Drawhill, Duke of Strafford, he, too, seemed calm.

"So much is clear between us," he said happily. "Later tonight I will seek the permission of your parents to call upon you in the near future."

She knew it was unecessary to point out to Trevor that neither parent was likely to approve his actual reason for wanting to see her again. Lust and selfishness would be clear as crystal, but the desire to pursue a friendship between a man and woman, a friendship that each of them needed and craved, must be a source of uncertainty and therefore of dismay.

"Frankly, Your Grace," she said blissfully, "I cannot imagine any difficulty, granting the use of discretion, in accomplishing the goal upon which we both are so determined."

Again they smiled warmly at each other. In only a few additional minutes she and Trevor had reached what they alone, and no one else in *le monde*, would call an understanding.

CHAPTER FOUR

"How marvelous it all was!" said Lady Fairfield on the following morning. She and her daughter were preparing to call upon a distant relative. Lady Fairfield had paused in deciding which of six cashmere shawls to wear over her dark satin cloak. "I see you as the Duchess of Strafford, lady of the manor in Kent but living well in London for the season."

"I hardly think that the Duke's request to call must foreshadow nuptials."

"Ah, the wedding, yes. I see it at St. Pancras, if they ever finish rebuilding the church. And I see a June reception in the garden, which is not *too* close to the graveyard, my dear."

"At the moment, Mamma, there is absolutely nothing between the Duke and myself that is in any way official."

"That will surely come later, Cammie. Otherwise—well, a gentleman would not want to waste your time."

Camilla had wondered whether or not she could at least hint to Mamma about the actual state of affairs between herself and the Duke, hoping to save Mamma from just such enthusiasms about her daughter's future and the depression that was certain to follow when her purpose and Trevor's became clear. But the quarrel that would instantly result offered too wearing a prospect for her to contemplate.

"Time, Mamma, will surely tell," she said pacifically.

Seated in his study Sir Osric looked away from his copy of Jimmy Wilson's newly founded weekly *The Economist*. Conversation with his favorite child was far pleasanter than puzzling about the intricacies of commerce.

"I am sure that you and Strafford will hit it off," Sir Osric said, proudly using an expression that was finding favor among youthful gentlemen in *le monde*. "A fine figure of a young man, Strafford is."

Camilla thought it only fair to tell him. "There is no reason to think that matters will go further between us."

"Indeed, I cannot see why they should if the two of you don't want them to."

Camilla smiled warmly at the sort of understanding response she expected from her father. But she had also come in to discuss her greatest worry of the moment.

"Mamma is already listening to marriage bells," she said. "I fear that if the—the worst happens, she will be deeply upset."

"You may be assured that I will clarify the matter for her after dinner, my dear."

"Thank you, Father, thank you."

Camilla was gratified and relieved as she left her father's study. As for Sir Osric, he settled down to decide exactly what words to use in telling Jimmy Wilson how fine and helpful a business weekly *The Economist* was, ignoring the fact that he could hardly understand three consecutive sentences. By the time he had evolved the most tactful phrases for a compliment that wasn't deserved from him, he had forgotten the entire conversation with Camilla. Dear Camilla.

Arthur was returning from a rout that had occupied a night and most of the following day. On the way up to his room he paused at sight of his younger sister descending the carpeted stairs.

"I hear that the Duke of Strafford will soon be calling," he said. Seeing her surprise, Arthur added, "The information was given to the brother of Sara Trowbridge, who had been at the point of setting her cap for him."

"The Duke will indeed be calling here."

"In that case, I hope you'll try to win him." He tapped her

on the shoulder the way he might have encouraged some child.

Camilla looked angry.

"Don't make faces at me." His lips briefly thinned even further than nature and heredity had intended. "I don't want my sister becoming known as what our statesmanlike paterfamilias would call a spinster without portfolio."

Camilla couldn't help being disappointed. In the past he had always been sympathetic, but at first sight of interest in her from a source considered suitable he had turned into a masculine version of their mother.

"I shall do only what I feel is correct," she said cuttingly, and walked off, leaving a somewhat discomposed brother on the stairs.

Camilla was looking forward to discussing the new development in her life with the only member of her immediate family who was not yet aware of it. No opportunity presented itself until the following day, when Louise, her older sister, entered the small sitting room where Camilla was disporting herself.

Putting her needlework aside, Camilla ran to embrace her. The affection was fully returned. Louise, a tall and stately young woman, was a year older than Camilla. She possessed their mother's hair, skin, and eyes, and their father's lips, forehead, and small nose. According to a family witticism, she had no features of her own.

Although she was married to a drunken wastrel, Louise would never admit as much, not even to her family. She put the best face on everything. Her only foible consisted of wearing virginal white down to her shoes, which Camilla regarded as an example of the wish being father to the thought.

"Everything is well with myself and Mr. Passy," she said automatically before she could be asked. "My dear father-in-law, the portrait painter, was knighted in the last honors list, making him Sir Victor. You can understand that as a result we are most excited."

"There has been a new development in my life as well." Without wasting many words, Camilla told about her seeing the Duke of Strafford and the peer's intention to call upon her during the next day, as he had apprised the Fairfields by a note in his hand.

"Is it possible that he will offer for you?" Louise was impressed. "The Duchess of Strafford! Won't some of your friends be envious!"

"We are being cordial and no more, he and I." It was vexing to get the same reaction from Louise as from everybody else in the family. "By seeing each other, he won't be pursued and I won't be bullied into marrying before I feel I should."

"But that seems hurtful to you," Louise protested. "Your time is taken in vain."

"I will be with someone whose presence pleases me and whom I please." Camilla looked away. "I would have expected you, of all women, to understand the urge to delay before setting one's course for life, to wait before marrying."

"I can assuredly sympathize with such an urge, my little friend," Louise said, reverting to a pet name she hadn't used in years. "But there are such good things in even an imperfect marriage that it is terrible to run the risk of perhaps missing those joys."

Camilla nodded respectfully, in the tradition of Sir Osric choosing not to make any disagreement public. She didn't appreciate hearing her older sister echoing Mamma's feelings in a different way, and Arthur's, and even the discreet Sir Osric's. At some time in the future she fully intended to be someone's bride. No one had been able to persuade her, directly or otherwise, not to spend tomorrow and the next few days or weeks pleasing herself—and the Duke of Strafford as well.

CHAPTER FIVE

The next day began pleasantly when the Duke called. In his canary waistcoat, white shirt with dark tie, dark trousers, and short ankle boots, Trevor Drawhill, the Duke of Strafford, seemed affable without losing the dignity that a peerage had imposed upon his natural sunny outlook. Camilla was delighted to hear him making sensible suggestions to her parents, and doing it with such ease that the elders' acceptance was taken for granted.

As a result, Camilla and her parents rode out with him for the annual running of the Gold Cup race at Ascot Heath in Berkshire. Sir Osric and Lady Fairfield, having for some obscure reason discarded their previous plans to attend the gala event, promptly performed a volte-face under Trevor's amiable prodding. He requested, too, that the family ride in his carriage, with its closed box and wine-red cushions over seats to match, and the glossy bay horses and the three men up.

The appointments delighted Lady Fairfield but caused no alteration in Sir Osric's normally polite demeanor. Arthur was not among those present, having informed his parents that he would spend the day in the company of friends.

Camilla found herself feeling completely at ease as she and the Duke smiled at each other and exchanged sentiments appropriate to feelings of warm politeness. Trevor, too, appeared to have been comforted by the presence of some member of the opposite sex acting as escort and without subtle schemes involving a future together.

The day at Ascot Heath was not sunny, but remained congenial for mid-June, as Camilla discovered upon their arrival. Flags flew in the Berkshire breeze. Men and women could be seen at the windows and on the balconies of nearby pavilions, especially the one that always reminded her of drawings that showed the Coliseum in Rome.

"The royal party should be arriving shortly," Trevor said as he led the way with Camilla to the Strafford box.

"And then the sun will shine," she murmured.

Trevor threw back his head and laughed. It was a response as different from her immediate family's as might well have been imagined. Mamma would have said that her younger daughter wasn't being respectful to the dear Queen. Sir Osric would have been sure to say discreetly that Camilla's point of view was interesting, and then wait for another subject that could be changed. Camilla was so astonished by this handsome peer's acceptance of her small witticism that she nearly halted in mid-stride. The Duke stopped himself from taking a further step and most likely causing a gout of mud to rise to the tip of Camilla's full azure skirt. Belatedly, and still wondering at the powerful response to what seemed a minor linguistic matter, she raised her skirt.

The quartet arrived at the Strafford holding just as the royal party was making its entrance at long last. Attended by the master and huntsmen of the Royal Buckhounds, the small woman and her stiff-backed consort settled themselves in the royal enclosure. There was a respectful silence in their vicinity.

Trevor looked across and down at the best-known couple in the kingdom. "Whenever I see them it occurs to me how contented they are in each other's presence. I am sure that their union was agreed upon in a rational and sensible atmosphere."

Camilla bridled. The Queen and her consort had often been held up to her as a couple whose happiness was the inevitable outcome of marriage.

"She is like a cow and he is a stuffed dummy," she said crisply, impelled further by her previous success as a wit.

Trevor responded only after a pause. "I would venture to

disagree. The Queen is well aware of her royal privileges and guards them jealously, which is far from a cowlike attitude. As for the Prince Consort, my impression after brief conversations is that he is a man who knows he could have been a success in statecraft if not for the marital choice which was made on his behalf."

Camilla was astonished once more at having been listened to and offered a considered answer. She felt herself growing a little weak in the knees, perhaps as a result.

Trevor must have misunderstood the expression that had briefly crossed her features. "Would you like a brisk canter about the grounds before the horses indulge?" he asked lightly.

She was still somewhat awestruck at his reactions to her. At the same time she couldn't help feeling that what he now wanted was to show her off to the families of eligible young women in hopes that he would not, as a result, find himself endlessly pursued. It was a goal with which she sympathized and largely shared, except that it was only her parents she wanted to impress. At the moment she was unable to act in concert with him.

"A little later, perhaps, if I may be allowed time to settle myself."

Her smile dispelled any feeling that he had encountered intractable opposition, as indeed he hadn't. Sighting a colleague from the Lords on the nearest path, he excused himself briefly and walked over.

Mamma, who had been listening to the most recent exchange between Camilla and "her" duke, misunderstood the reason for her daughter's hesitation.

"You look quite well, considering these new styles," Lady Fairfield said. "Be obliging to Trevor and stroll about with him."

Mamma pronounced the Duke's given name with the fervor of a soprano singer breasting some high note. As for her own costuming, she had reached an uneasy compromise with the current style by wearing only two petticoats beneath her russet merino. She remained proud of her figure as nature had conceived it and felt that a discreet showing could only keep up her spirits.

Camilla nodded at Lady Fairfield's request and said, "When he comes back I will join him in a walk around the premises."

"You are a good girl after all, Cammie. But then the prospect of marital happiness persuades any girl to cherish her family ties more deeply."

Camilla smiled but felt inwardly embarrassed. Because she was thwarting her mother's actual desires by spending so much time with a young man not seeking marriage to her, she found herself being more attentive to Mamma's wishes than usual.

True to her given word, when Trevor looked back she gestured her willingness to join him. He grinned in welcome at her approach. Mamma had just advised her against carrying one of the newly fashionable small white parasols and Camilla had obeyed, but the sight of other females flourishing that accessory caused her a certain regret.

Queen Victoria had decided against receiving in the royal enclosure, thereby departing from custom. The monarch's discourtesy made for a pleasanter afternoon in Camilla's jaundiced view. She found herself introducing Trevor to various social passersby with whom she was well acquainted.

"You seem to know a great many of society's mainstays," Trevor remarked during a lull.

"One of my useful accomplishments—don't you think?"

"Decidedly." His farsightedness indicated an opportunity to return the favor in part. "Would you now care to join a few notables with whom *I* am acquainted?"

"Of course."

At a turn Camilla knew that she was being observed by a darkly intense young man whose morning coat was a shade too long, whose pants were too dark for his complexion, hair, and eye coloring, and who mistakenly wore shiny lace-up shoes rather than short ankle boots. His dark eyes remained on her as she passed.

Trevor hadn't noticed the stranger, Camilla saw after a moment, his eyes resting on the friends at a distance. It was fortunate, she felt, that he hadn't seen the look of recognition directed at her by Will Royde, owner of the gambling hell on Bennet Street that she had visited while wearing a mask.

Forcing herself to concentrate on Trevor's mission, she greeted half a dozen young men and two wives whom she already knew, and permitted herself to be introduced to young men from Sussex and Kent. At the circle's center was William Arden, the second Baron Alvanley. Now in his fifties, a paunchy man, Alvanley was the perky wit who had been a particular friend of the late George Brummell in the heyday of Prince George's Regency. It happened to be the subject he was discussing, making sad comparisons to these current days.

"In George's time a woman could be seen in public and displaying all the delights of her figure," Alvanley was saying to a Sussex man, evidently continuing a discussion previously begun. He would have found Lady Fairfield a congenial spirit. "Gambling was winked at, and taking two drinks in succession didn't draw a frown from any hostess. Roistering was almost a public pastime, while a young man with any rake's impulses these days must needs first turn his collar around and foist himself on some servant girl. I realize full well that I am older now and not disposed to think of younger men taking their pleasures, but the changes I see on all sides are most infernally distasteful."

Trevor had, of course, been weighing the elder's words. "My strong feeling is that anything that could be done in George's Regency can now be done as well, provided appropriate discretion is observed."

"But why should a man have to be discreet and hypercritical, to live one sort of life in private and another in public? I am the first to admit that butter has often melted in my mouth. A man should be known to his equals with warts and all, rather than having to dissemble."

Camilla was plainly not intended to take part in this conversation. She couldn't resist looking past the circle and down the path. William Royde had followed for part of the way. His dark eyes were turned almost voraciously on her. It was impossible to see him and not dread the prospect of his entering this talk, then identifying Camilla as a masked visitor to his place of business.

She brushed Trevor on an arm, a gesture that was observed by two of the young men. "Please excuse me, Your Grace, while I briefly return to my parents. I had forgotten to leave a message with them."

"I will be happy to accompany you, as the race is going to be under way before very long."

"There is no immediate need, I do assure you." She smiled wickedly. "Who would be so base as to take a gentleman away from any discussion of his privileges?"

Alvanley, to his credit, laughed with the others.

As she ventured forth, she overheard someone say that the horses would soon be parading single file to the starting point. It meant that the Duke was going to be joining her in minutes at the Strafford box. Royde, if he chose to talk with her, wouldn't have much time. It was an advantage from her view.

Nevertheless she made a point of half-circling the immediate area. At the very least Royde wouldn't be in almost a direct path to her destination. Trevor was an attentive listener but not often an observant walker and wouldn't see any dealings of hers with the unsavory William Royde.

"Miss Fairfield." Royde had moved with swiftness and was bad-manneredly in front of her rather than at a side. The thick brows were lowered as if to help convey his feeling of urgency. "I had not been able to reach you before."

"What does this mean, sir?" She would deny whatever he might say about knowing her, deny it good-humoredly or with haughtiness, as the occasion demanded. "I am not aware of ever having met you before."

"Miss Fairfield, you know who I am and what I do to earn my bread and salt."

If she had wanted to fence with him verbally, one look at his rigid posture might have led her to point out that he had obviously received some training from the Army. Perhaps he was one of those who had been unable to purchase a commission. Otherwise he might have become a gallant soldier of Queen Vicky rather than the officially despised proprietor of an illicit establishment.

"More importantly at this time," he added, promptly confirming her worst suspicions, "I know that you are Lady Fortune."

It was the name by which someone had called her at Bennet Street after she had touched the backs of cards for good fortune, which had indeed materialized for some.

"I recall reading that sobriquet in one of the papers of society gossip," she said, frowning ostentatiously. There had indeed been a discussion of her anonymous activities in *Day's Doings*, the organ of society tattle. "I cannot conceive what it has to do with me."

The humorless Royde didn't smile, but he must have realized she was actually asking how she had been found out.

"A number of my patrons spoke to me of the matter and one of them suggested with amusement that the description of a bright-haired girl with blue eyes resembled that of his sister. I made a point of seeing you to decide for myself, and now I am certain that my patron was correct."

At some time in the near future, Camilla told herself, she would talk to Arthur about the perils of offering too many speculations.

"As I recollect, the creature to whom you refer by that appalling name was masked."

"It would be impossible to see you and hear you speak without being certain."

She didn't know whether or not she had been praised for comeliness and decided to pass over the implications of his remark. Her expression didn't change.

Royde flushed at her coolness, which told Camilla what she had briefly wanted to know. He must have been well aware that any personal relations between them were out of the question. But he almost certainly couldn't conceive that it was his humorless pomposity that would have put off even a more free-minded young woman. Such snobbishness of manner was more inflexible than that of anyone in the circles she knew.

"You helped my burgeoning career greatly on that night," he added. "I have been beholden to you ever since. Many a patron has come to my place to see Lady Fortune and has stayed to gamble. Others have returned for that purpose and they, too, have swelled my coffers. By which I mean—"

She interrupted what would have been a prolix clarification of a phrase with which she was already familiar.

"And this creature who resembles—has she not materialized again?"

He didn't choose to give the answer that she certainly knew. "I have requested of several female acquaintants that they put on hairpieces of a similar color and pretend that they are Lady Fortune. None of the females has carried the slightest conviction."

Camilla lowered her eyes before realizing that the moment of modesty would have given away her guilt if nothing else did.

"Really, sir, I cannot deny too forcefully that I am the creature to whom you refer."

And that, to be sure, was the strict truth.

"I have sought you out to express the hope that you will care to return to my establishment and do again what you did on that night. I can assure you that no questions would be asked, no further attempt made to seek you out when you aren't masked."

She was not at all tempted, her time now being taken up largely by the pleasures of being in the same company with Trevor. Even had she wanted to make added forays into the lower depths, common sense would have kept her from it. If Royde could speak with her after one appearance and determine her identity, it was possible that someone—a gossip collector for *Day's Doings*, for example—might achieve the same result.

"Should you wish some private acknowledgment of your efforts, I will be glad to make a contribution to any charitable cause that Lady Fortune names. Let us say fifty pounds—no, guineas, fifty guineas, for every night on which she appears."

"Let us say instead that the matter is closed."

"Not that, Miss Fairfield, but in abeyance and awaiting your further consideration."

He was telling her quite clearly that he would seek her out at some time in the near future when he might be able to provide further reasons for Camilla to agree—and possibly destroy her social standing.

She turned away, not trusting herself to speak further, and hurried off.

CHAPTER SIX

The horses appeared to trudge into the start of their race with what looked to Camilla like a concerted attempt to dismay the finest of British society. Only at the three-quarter mark, however, did the animals apparently choose to attempt a burst of speed. Camilla found herself feeling excited by the sight, her left hand raised tautly. She felt a stronger hand firmly enclosing it. Trevor Drawhill, sportsman though he was, had noted her response and was taking time to offer a friendly smile just before the conclusion of the race.

"Thank you," she said, surprised by the unaccustomed shyness in her tones. "The comfort was much appreciated."

"As I have just lost ten pounds in a wager, Miss Fairfield, you are not the only one in need of soothing."

She took part of his warm, strong hand in hers and bore down briefly upon it.

"If I could have anticipated the warmth of your reaction, Miss Fairfield, I would have arranged to lose twenty pounds."

"A wager of ten pounds makes you seem venturesome, but a wager of twenty would have been rash."

Even as they smiled at each other, Camilla was struck by her own choice of words, the concern over a man with no long-lasting interest in her. It was as if somewhere in the recesses of her mind Camilla Fairfield for once was thinking quite rashly herself.

The balance of the afternoon passed pleasantly enough. Congratulations were offered by losers and received by winners. The skills of every horse were praised and those of the jockeys sneered at. The moist track, it was inevitably decided, was responsible for all of the day's setbacks, none of which could have been anticipated.

In the fullness of time the Duke returned his guests to the Fairfield home on Lower Brook Street. Very possibly he sensed that Lady Fairfield was too weary to make herself an effective chaperone in case he chose to enter the domicile. His decision to leave was enough to sadden Camilla in spite of gaining her reluctant approval.

As he made his farewells to Camilla's parents, she was able to understand why he seemed so contented. The visit to Ascot had firmly given the effect he wanted. To everyone who counted in *le monde* it must now be perfectly clear that he had chosen a female companion for a while, at the very least, and could not at this time be seeking another.

When he paused in front of her, it was almost as if he had some genuine feeling for Camilla. The palm of his right hand was touching hers with a certain earned familiarity.

"I shall take the liberty of writing to Sir Osric shortly about matters of interest to us both." His splendid eyes were looking directly into hers.

She couldn't help telling herself a little scornfully that he must be a consummate thespian.

"I anticipate another reunion," she said quietly, and looked away before she had meant to do so.

She was occupied on the next afternoon by a ride along Hyde Park with a female friend who called in a *vis-à-vis* carriage. Her friend was so much concerned with details of her forthcoming marriage that she asked no questions whatever about Camilla's being squired by the Duke of Strafford. It was a pleasant time nevertheless.

Arriving back at home, she found Mamma up in the small sitting room and deeply engaged before the writing desk with a quill and a sheet of gray foolscap.

"The coachmen will need new livery and prices are scandalous," she was saying as she looked up. "Thompson's in Oxford Street, at the servants' bazaar, is the place where the Marchioness of Dover sends her footmen. As for Annie, she, too, will need new costuming if she is to accompany us. I must send her to Cox on Marlborough Road. She has rarely needed such attention over twenty years, although there are times when I think she has set herself upon the life's work of eating your dear father out of house and home."

Camilla forebore to point out that Annie's duties about the house would certainly put considerable restraint on age-induced *embonpoint*. Mamma's sudden energy was of greater interest.

"Cammie, dear, your father has received a missive from the Duke of Strafford, and the family is invited—all but Louise, to be sure—for a weekend at his home in Kent."

Mamma waited to see an expression of happiness cross her daughter's face. Camilla, however, did nothing more than chuckle. News of such an invitation would make it conclusive to any remaining doubters that the two of them must be involved in the rituals of courtship. It was the response that both craved from all those who wanted to feel sure that neither could draw a breath without some partner on hand to be critical of the other for breathing in a shallow manner. This, to Camilla's occasionally cynical mind, was what others considered as living happily ever after.

"There is no time for each of us to buy a complete wardrobe, Cammie, but I do think that a dress for the evening would be most suitable to you. However, you must not attempt the excesses of these infernal new styles in evening wear. A neckline that plunges only slightly can be attractive. A deep plunge is something that a man likes to see in the clothing of strange women, but not, to be sure, in a girl for whom he intends to offer."

"He hasn't indicated any plans to do so," Camilla said quickly.

It wasn't surprising that Mamma should jump gleefully to the first available conclusion. Camilla had expected nothing less since shortly after she and Strafford began playing their social game. Now that she could see the results before her, however, Camilla was edgy and uncomfortable at building up Mamma's hopes.

Lady Fairfield paid slight attention to disclaimers.

"As I see matters, Cammie," she said, encouraging her daughter to look on the brightest side, "Strafford wants you to become familiar with the home where he was born and meet his longtime friends as well as his mother, the Dowager Duchess. Following which you may be quite sure of the results. I want you to promise that you will be modest and discreet."

In a voice lowered by shame, which Mamma fortunately didn't identify, Camilla promised.

"You must not be servile in any way, but, on the other hand, you should not rise to possible provocations." Mamma might have been conceiving the treatment she would mete out to any girl who ensnared her son. "I don't want the Dowager Duchess to think of you as shrewish *or* meek."

Further plans were made before Camilla could say another word. Mamma, her small nostrils twitching with anticipation, now felt that a wedding at dear Trevor's home or his parish church would help establish Camilla with the locals, as she condescendingly called those men and women away from London with whom Trevor had been raised. At least one or more of Trevor's female relations must be among the bridesmaids, further entrenching Cammie in the family's good graces. On a fresh sheet of gray foolscap a note to that effect was made accordingly.

Camilla would have been unable to put in any words at this time. Lady Fairfield spoke more and more grandiloquently. Notes were added at a furious clip. It seemed not to make any difference whether Camilla would be happy in matrimony or the man would turn into a useless and impractical fool, as had taken place with her older sister's husband. It was an issue to be ignored at first and then papered over in case of need. Mamma simply didn't care.

Sadly Camilla looked down at the graying head bent over foolscap sheets. Lady Fairfield was neither unkind nor foolish, but felt that her daughter must be like every girl in London and obtain what was considered best for her. Camilla didn't think that she wanted to make any explanations now. Lady Fairfield was actually responding to another human being's good feelings by making every attempt to stifle them. Not for the first time Camilla found herself feeling both angry and affectionate while in her mother's presence.

She resolved the dilemma by murmuring that it was necessary to change for supper, and that she would soon be back for further discussions. Just as she reached the creaky top step to the second floor, she heard her brother's door opening slowly.

Arthur eased himself into the hall. Only the blink of his large eyes was rapid. One hand held onto the gaudy white doorknob as if for dear life.

"Cammie, is the house in motion?" he whispered.

"It is not," Camilla said firmly, distracted from her own thoughts.

"Slightly, perhaps? An inch or so in any direction whatever? No? Well, in a way, in a manner of speaking, you have relieved my mind."

That was the opposite of the feeling she had planned on raising in him. She fixed her eyes forbiddingly on his thin lips. "Your mouth doesn't look large, but in the presence of William Royde it becomes quite cavernous. That is a miracle of nature I hope to discuss with you if ever you are *compos mentis.*"

"Not at this time, Cammie." He shuddered strongly. "Even if I knew what you were talking about, I would not want to use my intellect excessively at this time."

Recollections of past arguments stirred in her. It was useless to tell him about Royde having identified her because of Arthur's talking too much. Arthur would simply chuckle and say something dismissive. He always did when rebuked. As a rule he expected his trespasses to be forgiven. Many a time, discussing his drinking and lechery and gambling, she had gnashed her teeth in envy only because he had been granted liberties at birth as a male.

"You, I take it, will not be among those present at supper," she said as a preliminary to going about her business.

Arthur put up a hand before his mouth and kept it there a moment before speaking again. "Now, really, we must not talk about food. A sack of posset might be tempting, though. Indeed, I can think of no other beverage I have never sampled, and that only because it's virtually extinct. But no food. Definitely no food."

She was tempted to sarcasm by his needless explanation. "You, my dear brother, will be the attraction to all eyes when we reach Kent."

"What on earth are you talking about now?"

"We—the family, except for Louise and the husband you so much resemble, I believe—have been invited to Kent for a weekend with the Duke of Strafford."

"I expect to be indisposed. Not to put too fine a point upon it, I devoutly hope to be indisposed." He would have smiled if the energy had been in him at this time. "Mother can look after your interests."

Camilla said promptly, "I would like you to come."

Even as the words were being spoken, it crossed her mind that his presence could indeed be useful. Arthur's typical behavior might well account for the Duke not offering for Camilla as Mamma confidently expected. Even a reason that was likely to bring reluctant agreement from her was preferable to a rejection that seemed without motive. Otherwise Lady Fairfield might become distraught, a fate which Camilla certainly didn't wish on her mother.

"*I? Away from le monde?*" Arthur's speech was becoming clipped, as happened when he anticipated feeling uncomfortable.

"You will help show the Duke and his mother that we are a solid and united family."

"Oh, I'd hardly be an asset. Not in strangers' eyes. Not to country bumpkins."

It was true. Camilla's reasoning powers indicated another persuasive argument.

"You owe me some favors, Arthur. Do this one for me in return."

"*I* owe you favors? Nary a one."

"Oh yes, you do." Lightness of tone could be more influential with her jittery brother than an itemized list. "Many a time I could have crept into your room when you were asleep and hit you with a fireplace iron. I have refrained. With heroic self-denial I have kept from making a deep impression on you."

"I? The best brother a gel could possibly have. The noblest."

"Most seriously, Arthur, I would very much appreciate your joining the family for this expedition."

"Very well. I suppose there are some favors I do owe you. And there may be added ones I will need. In the future."

"Thank you, Arthur."

"You won't thank me afterwards. Shall get drunk. Be sauced all weekend. Sneak up with the stuff to whatever kennel I'm allotted and I'll drown my tongue."

"Arthur, I can only trust your better nature to assert itself."

But as she left him Camilla confidently expected his desire for social approval to lie dormant when the time came, as usual.

CHAPTER SEVEN

In describing the weekend visit as an expedition, Camilla had not been making any noticeable error. Preparations along the line of intensive packing were enough to consume most days of the preceding week. It had been decided by Mamma that the family cabriolet should be kept in town and a four-wheeled wagonette borrowed from Louise's father-in-law, the affluent and frequently unbearable Sir Victor. Negotiations with the distinguished portrait painter were ultimately successful but consumed several long days for Sir Osric and involved his greatest reserves of diligence and diplomacy.

The packing of luggage boxes began in earnest some three days before departure. Added time was spent by Mamma in giving needless instructions to the family butler, the infallible Blackhouse, who accepted them equably.

As if these duties were not sufficiently taxing, Mamma further occupied herself by pleading and cajoling Arthur to be on his best behavior in the difficult times that lay immediately ahead. The young man was undoubtedly stirred by Mamma's repeated conviction that he was blessed with innate goodness and decency. Camilla, speaking to him at various times in the days before departure, found her confidence in his recklessness beginning to waver. All the same, she continued to hope for the worst. In her youthful cynicism she believed that every silver lining has a cloud.

The wagonette, modeled on one that had been recently introduced by the Prince Consort, offered room for each family member to inspect the discomfort of two others. Space

intended for wine and ice was occupied only by air. Arthur
made a point of looking away from that particular section of
this capacious vehicle.

While Sir Osric spoke knowledgeably about fishing in the
Darent River and the uses of the Romney marshes, Mamma
urged her daughter to behave winningly with the Duke. Camilla listened at first, assured Mamma that her manners
would be impeccable, then stopped listening.

Arthur, responding to their father's given store of information about the area, said, "Jolly. Very jolly." More and more
his clipped speech was beginning to remind Camilla of that
noted literary figure Mr. Jingle dealing with some confused
members of the Pickwick Club.

Annie, the maid, sitting to one side and not involved in any
conversation, looked ahead stolidly and sometimes glanced
out a window. If she knew that Camilla envied her for the
length of this excursion, the longtime servant gave no sign of
it.

The village of Strafford lurked in wait not far from Swanley.
Trevor's house could be reached only across a broad lawn
defaced with artificially colored trees, rustic furniture, a three-
tiered fountain (now inactive), and an immobile goat cart.
The commodious-looking house, which came in sight after
the third flowering urn in a row, was in the Gothic Revival
manner.

"We are the Fairfields," Sir Osric told the impassive butler,
who had promptly answered his ring.

"Please enter," said that deep-voiced factotum. "My name
is Cupples. I hope that your journey was not too arduous."

The hall was overpowering without being large. A staircase
led down to a sofa below a stained glass window, with paint-
ings of foliage and birds looking less attractive than they did
in the real life not far off. Camilla hoped that the decoration
reflected the tastes of the late Duke, Trevor's father.

Mamma was the last to join them, having paused to make
certain that Annie and the coachmen would be disposed of at
various strategic points about the house. She was first, how-

ever, to trust her bonnet to Cupples, whereupon Camilla followed, and the men divested themselves of their bowlers.

"Please follow me to the sitting room, where the Dowager Duchess will be joining all her guests shortly."

Camilla would have preferred to refresh herself after the long ride, but assumed that the immediate greeting of guests was a custom of rural England. This time it was Mamma who led the way. The drawing room was furnished with a deep carpet, stiff chairs, floor lamps with red glass in fluted shades, a fireplace with a wide screen, and two matching sofas. On one of these a pair of females of different ages were sitting warily.

"I am Mrs. Winifred Malbot," the older one offered. She was a plain woman in similar clothes, and hardly in the London fashion. "I am the aunt of Miss Vivien Malbot here."

The younger one was a fair-skinned, redheaded girl with merry eyes. Her walking dress, of amber crepe, was also out of fashion in London and had certainly received considerable use. It had been cared for, however, and still looked becoming. At sight of Miss Malbot's wholesome appearance, so different from types to which he had become accustomed in *le monde*, Arthur drew in a deep breath.

"My niece has returned for one weekend in order to see the home she visited when she was younger," Mrs. Malbot said. "Vivien was a childhood playmate of the Duke's."

Mamma narrowed her eyes at hearing those almost proprietorial tones. Clearly the wholesome Vivien was a rival for Trevor's paw in marriage. Camilla, having now been vouchsafed one more reason for the invitation to have been tendered, subdued a smile.

Mamma said, "You were not invited down by the Duke!"

"By the Dowager Duchess, who certainly speaks for him."

Mamma nodded, relieved as one source of possible tension suddenly evaporated. Any mother's choice for the position of daughter-in-law wasn't necessarily that of the son. Nevertheless Mamma adopted the goal of causing the others to lose confidence in Vivien's ability to win the Duke to her side.

The smile she turned to Vivien was palpably false, at least to her daughter's eyes. "My dear, you look so lovely in that walking dress that I wish it was still all the crack in London."

Vivien only smiled. Mrs. Malbot's newly frozen demeanor would have been appropriate for a statue that had been unaccountably overlooked by the late Lord Elgin at the Parthenon.

"We are not in London now," she said, realizing that the pause ought to be filled by a parry to counter the other matron's thrust.

"No, but dear Trevor is in and out of *le monde,* as we indigenous inhabitants call it, and is able to make fitting comparisons."

"Clothes are like people," Mrs. Malbot returned. "It is the quality that matters."

Sir Osric cleared his throat, preparing to soothe ruffled feathers. As had happened before in Camilla's experience, he delayed long enough for somebody else to speak.

Vivien Malbot said, "My aunt and I, like yourselves, are here as guests." Her pleasant voice was bereft of the nasal tones that Londoners like Arthur associated with those from the outland.

Mamma was prepared to accept the olive branch with words but reject it in any action. Camilla, knowing Lady Fairfield well, spoke first, and with unmistakable sincerity.

"I hope that we will all spend a pleasant few days here," she said, drawing out both hands.

Vivien clasped them as an indication of genuine amiability. Mamma's smile at this sight was not heartfelt, causing Mrs. Winifred Malbot to resume her splendid impersonation of an Elgin marble.

The door to the room suddenly opened, but it was not the Dowager Duchess or her son who entered.

"The family bid me to inform you that they will be delayed," Cupples intoned as if it were a psalm. "They look forward to greeting you before supper."

By the time Camilla joined her family in the upstairs sitting room, she had put on the new dress for evening wear. It was in azure, with a low neckline and shoulders visible. She had rubbed slivers of burnt wood against her lashes to darken them attractively, but scorned to massage stiff paper against her cheeks and thereby simulate a reddish glow which came naturally to her new friend.

Mamma, inspecting her daughter, pronounced the results to be satisfactory on the whole. She felt that Camilla had been clever in responding pleasantly to the other aspirant for the title of Duchess of Strafford.

"I meant every word," Camilla protested. "I decline to argue with or devil Vivien Malbot."

"And very clever of you," Mamma repeated, missing the point completely. "Always make a good impression, but keep an eye out."

Arthur, walking quietly into the room, said, "I agree with part of that. About making a good impression."

"There's a first time for everything," Camilla said blithely. "Mamma feels that we shouldn't consort with the enemy."

"It is the least I could actually do. For my own flesh and blood, that is."

"What do you mean?" Mamma asked tentatively.

Arthur gave an irritable shrug. He had watched the near-hostilities downstairs as if only one person was in the large sitting room, and that was the redheaded Vivien. Never before could he remember seeing a girl who looked so sweet, so gracious, so confident in her own abilities. Here was a girl with whom he felt it urgent to become better acquainted.

"I have a plan about Miss Malbot," Arthur said, telling part of the truth with practiced skill. "Perhaps I can attract her to myself. Only for the length of our stay, of course. Then she will see little of the Duke. Camilla's path to an offer is certain to be smoothed."

Lady Fairfield promptly approved the suggestion, in part because it emanated from her son.

"What an excellent stratagem!" she said enthusiastically.

Camilla kept from expressing further shock at her brother's unprecedented willingness to oblige any living creature, let alone a member of his immediate family. Nor did she say that his help wasn't actually required, as the so-called rivalry between two girls was nonexistent. One look at Arthur's glowing features, his quick movements, and she understood that he had been smitten. No girl like the rurally raised Vivien had ever been in his view before, and the propinquity was enough to draw his lively interest.

She shrugged. It was a development she couldn't have expected, and might cause Mamma to be more vexed at the Duke's failure to make any offer for the maiden who ostensibly returned his interest in her. But the matter could only be dealt with at such a time as it reached the surface, not before.

"And now," said Sir Osric, echoing his daughter's feelings, "let us make our way downward and resume the hunt. I believe I faintly discerned a view halloo despite the season, and our quarry is very nearly in sight."

CHAPTER EIGHT

"How pleasant that you could all be here with us," the Dowager Duchess of Strafford beamed. "Trevor and I both look forward to a couple of delightful days."

The guests smiled back in return, all with varying degrees of bonhomie. Camilla, glancing at the faces of those who stood nearest to her, restrained a wide smile. The Duke's gravity was equally suspicious. Looking away from the stylishly dressed Trevor, whom she silently rejoiced upon seeing, Camilla's eyes met those of the Dowager Duchess. Whether the woman was well disposed towards her or not, Camilla found it impossible to know at this time.

The dining room doors opened and that magisterial butler Cupples appeared.

The Dowager Duchess said, "Supper is most assuredly ready for us. And not a moment too soon, in my stomach's considered opinion."

Camilla was able to smile sincerely now and not be suspected of sarcasm. The Dowager Duchess was a woman in her mid-fifties. Her nose was large, her eyes small, but as a young woman her figure must have been a challenge to any male. She wore gray with becoming touches of white, scorning fashion for a costume that looked well on her. It was a disposition she shared with Vivien, and probably made Mamma a little uncomfortable to see. Like her son, the Dowager Duchess had been blessed with more intelligence than most, although it may have taken different forms in her case.

Adroitly using her privileges as a hostess, she offered a

hand to Sir Osric, who joined her to lead the way into the dining room.

Trevor said tactfully to Mrs. Malbot, "Tomorrow evening, if you permit, I will have the pleasure of escorting you to the festive board."

Mrs. Malbot looked restless as Trevor joined Lady Fairfield.

Arthur, who might have been expected to act as escort for the remaining older woman, approached Vivien instead in order to gain even the momentary pleasure of her company.

Camilla was left to walk with Mrs. Winifred Malbot. The older woman spoke not a word as they entered the spacious dining room. Just before they were to disperse to their assigned places, she remembered her manners.

"As you haven't shown me the least discourtesy, Miss Fairfield, you don't deserve any such treatment at my hands."

Camilla, taken aback by the graceful apology, returned a smile. Mrs. Malbot didn't need to add that the pressures of finding a suitable husband for Vivien were forcing her into disagreeable behavior that she almost certainly loathed in herself.

"No lasting offense has been given," Camilla responded warmly and accurately. "I do assure you."

Mrs. Winifred Malbot chuckled at the younger female's honesty. It occurred to Camilla that in another situation the two of them might have been friends.

As the guests settled themselves, Camilla saw Lady Fairfield glowering at Mrs. Winifred Malbot, as if the other woman's speaking with her fair daughter was an unforgivable offense. Camilla felt a little ashamed for Mamma, but at least there was no discussion of the matter.

Mrs. Malbot now proceeded to nearly dissipate Camilla's warm feelings for her. It happened that Vivien had been placed beside the Dowager Duchess, on the one hand, and Arthur, on the other. At sight of the seating arrangement, which couldn't possibly favor her niece discoursing with Trevor, she irritated all the others by rising abruptly.

"I do think that Vivien is so tired she must return to her room immediately for a rest."

"That would be unfortunate," Trevor said easily. "I had hoped to converse with Vivien after the repast."

At this assurance Mrs. Malbot looked mollified and sat down again, pretending that the change was reluctantly made. Now it was Arthur's turn to be displeased, but he remained silent. Camilla found her own lips pursed disapprovingly, then realized that Trevor was setting himself to placate both sets of fractious family.

The Dowager Duchess, assisting him, launched into a discussion about the quality of the turtle soup with which the meal began. Given Sir Osric's deft aid, she drew others into judicious assessments of the oyster patties which followed. Camilla joined in cheerfully when it came to dissecting the *fricandeau* of veal, of which she highly approved. Lady Fairfield discoursed about a supper at the home of the dear Duke of Wellington some time ago, not failing to mention that Wellington had called Camilla a beauty. Mrs. Malbot was impelled to speak of a *sauce tomate*, which Vivien had been taught by her late mother to prepare skillfully, and added that the capacity to ensure that meals would be cooked well was worth far more than mere mechanical attractiveness, which would fade with time. As for Vivien and Arthur, they were content to look at each other and ignore most of the delicious comestibles in front of them.

Trevor had only given Camilla an occasional conspiratorial smile, in the meantime making himself agreeable to Mrs. Malbot on his other hand. Camilla, now well aware of the demands of his position as host, was amused to see him at it.

Mrs. Malbot waited until the supper was finished, the charlotte russe cleared from every plate, the cheese *soufflé à la vanille* out of sight, and the gold-rimmed cups only half filled with the green tea that had been known in her girlhood and Lady Fairfield's and the Dowager Duchess's as Regent's Punch. Only then did she return to the fray.

"I am sure that you want to talk with Vivien now, Trevor, as you promised."

"Indeed yes, once we have left the arena of dirty crockery."

He smiled across the table, pleased that Vivien was occupied in talking to Arthur.

"And afterwards," Mrs. Malbot continued remorselessly, not having noticed where her niece's attentions lay, "I feel sure that Vivien can be prevailed upon to favor us at the pianoforte. I am sure you recall that she plays beautifully."

Lady Fairfield, as if on cue, said, "Camilla has a quite noteworthy musical accomplishment in her singing voice, having been trained by the great signor Amadeo Bertolozzi of Milan himself. You doubtless know how much he helped educate the great Madame Vestris."

Camilla flinched. Certainly she was able to carry a simple tune, but believed she did it only with slight adequacy. It was a social accomplishment best kept private, in her own view.

"Camilla's singing voice should be quite a discovery to you," Lady Fairfield added brightly. "It is yet another facet of her nature, and not overfamiliar to you after many, many years."

Mrs. Malbot reared back at this open declaration of silken hostilities. "I believe that in simple justice my Vivien alone should perform tonight."

This challenge, too, was accepted. "I fail to see any justice whatever in such an arrangement," Lady Fairfield snapped.

Camilla was aware of Trevor's briefly pursed lips and found herself feeling sympathy for the beleaguered young gallant. No passing moment could have shown more clearly why he had suggested that he and Camilla pretend to be attracted to one another, or why she had so eagerly agreed.

Sir Osric, the experienced tactician, said, "I cannot help feeling that the best course to follow at this moment is for us to take a brief stroll along the grounds. It is certainly necessary in order to settle such a repast."

Trevor agreed immediately and gratefully, as did the Dowager Duchess. The older women relapsed into sullen silence. Vivien remained deep in conversation with Arthur, and only her aunt's clarion call made it plain that she was to get up from the table. Taking advantage of Vivien's interest being elsewhere, Trevor stood slightly back of Camilla and waited for her to join him.

It was soon decided by the older women that cloaks would be worn by all the females for a venture into the fresh air. The males, scorning such cover, were left in the large sitting room. Sir Osric and Trevor discussed the possible size of their contributions to the Guy's Hospital Football Club, which had just been founded in London. Arthur, dazed by recollections of the enchanting Vivien, offered no enlightenment whatever.

Camilla, approaching the staircase to her room, saw the invaluable Cupples leaving the presence of the Dowager Duchess. The older woman was now encased in a sturdy dark cloth apparatus which did duty as a cloak. Camilla complimented her upon the dark coloring, which highlighted her complexion and brought out the shade of her eyes.

The Dowager Duchess smiled. "Do you truly consider that it brings out such beauty as is left to me?"

Her head was cocked at an angle, indicating that her acuity may have been at least equal to Trevor's. Camilla was not inclined to game with her.

"Its modishness could be improved."

"At my time of life honesty is preferable to kindness." This second smile was less mechanical, more genuine. "Trevor informs me—belatedly, I fear—that he finds you interesting."

"I am, of course, pleased to know of this."

"He did not apprise me until I had issued invitations to Winifred and dear Vivien, of whom I am fond. I tell you this because I did not intend for my son to be the object of a battle royal."

"Ma'am, I can understand that." Such frankness deserved a similar response. "I expect that you favor Miss Malbot in this matter."

"I have been acquainted with Vivien's family since before she was born, as you may be aware." The Dowager Duchess shrugged. "The daughter-in-law you know is more restful to contemplate than the daughter-in-law you don't."

The purposeful misquotation, the friendly sharing of a pleasantry, caught Camilla by surprise and then shamed her.

Once again she had gained the liking of an older woman, another who was certain to be distressed because of the game that she and Trevor were playing.

"At the moment I am wary," the Dowager Duchess added in response to Camilla's recent indirect question. "But I could be persuaded otherwise."

Camilla tried to look pleased but found herself wondering if there would be any other victims of this cheeky but understandable lark. Without regretting for a moment what she and Trevor had already done to simplify their lives, she didn't think she could calmly accept one more jot of warmth as a result, one more hand offered in friendship.

Vivien was inspecting herself in the cheval glass in her room. The cloak of Irish poplin which she wore was a suitable garment for country nights but could possibly cause a raised eyebrow in cosmopolitan London. It was a consideration that she had never encountered, and she found it unsettling.

For much of the past year she had been feeling unsettled. Over a period of twenty months she had been engaged to Lieutenant Athelney Gregson of the Tenth Light Dragoons. An accident that involved a cannon which slipped its moorings had killed her Athelney. Despair and grief occupied her for several months, and then one of her Malbot cousins had pointed out crisply that she was young and alive, and that it was necessary for a female to settle down with a spouse.

"I can never marry now," Vivien could recall saying.

"You must." The Malbot cousin stared. "Tuck your red hair into a country cap and set it for some wealthy man. You will soon be his wife, unless he has previously made other plans."

"I could not be happy."

"You must make the attempt," her cousin said dryly.

One of her Kilburn connections knew that Trevor Drawhill remained maritally unoccupied. As she and Trevor had liked each other during childhood, and as Trevor earned five hundred pounds a year in rent rolls and occupied a seat in the Lords as well, his suitability as a husband was worth investigating in greater detail. Aunt Malbot had arranged invitations for them both. The journey from Sittingbourne had been wearing but not difficult.

Trevor, it seemed, had recently found another young lady, and in this one he was keenly interested. Vivien herself had become intrigued by Arthur Fairfield, who was not only devilish handsome but seemed truly sophisiticated. He was unlike any male she had ever known, so that it was impossible to make comparisons unfair to him. It was as if she had been born all over again and had just discovered the pleasures of being courted by a worldly cosmopolite like Arthur.

Looking at herself a little longer in the cloak as reflected by the glass in her guest room, Vivien wished she had obeyed her Aunt Malbot's urgent injunctions and purchased clothes that were currently acceptable in London.

She was trying to fit the cloak more tightly around her in hopes that it would seem imposing, when her Aunt Malbot knocked twice at the door and entered. Mrs. Winifred Malbot was wearing a cashmere shawl, which she insisted was enough for all the night protection she ever needed in summer.

"You have been ignoring Trevor," Aunt Malbot said a little sharply.

"He has found someone else."

"What you must do, then, is to take Trevor away from Miss Fairfield."

Vivien was going to remark that she wasn't aware of how to proceed on such a mission. She stopped herself, having realized that if Arthur Fairfield had been inclined toward another charmer, the mission would have been performed speedily. Because of her farm experience, Vivien immediately thought how much these things depended on the matter of whose ox was being gored. Like the well-raised girl she was, Vivien blushed afterwards.

"It may be too late to attract Trevor to another girl, and especially to one he has known since early youth."

She didn't add that she, too, felt that a marriage along those lines would be sorely lacking in adventure. How could she blame Trevor for feeling that way? Now that she had met

Arthur, the craving for fresh experiences was rising strongly in her.

"No, that might not be," Aunt Malbot said, having given fresh thought to the matter. "Without knowing it, you may have adopted the right course to gain his interest."

"What do you mean?"

"By pretending that you're attracted to the other fellow, you could make Trevor feel pangs of jealousy."

"I don't think that Trevor has looked in my direction long enough to feel anything but friendship towards a childhood companion."

"Perhaps if you keep on with the girl's brother the tide will turn."

Vivien smiled now. "I will do my best to follow the course you advocate, dear Aunt."

CHAPTER NINE

"I have spent more time with you," said Vivien Malbot when the promenade across the Strafford grounds began, "than with any other in the house."

Ahead of them and out of earshot, as Arthur confirmed with a quick glance, Cammie and the Duke were walking alongside the Fairfield elders. Mrs. Malbot and the Dowager Duchess kept a good distance behind. It was possible to talk with a certain amount of freedom, as Vivien had previously noted.

"You've never met me before," Arthur pointed out. "So many things about me that you must want to know. And vice versa. Very much vice versa."

"Couldn't *I* feel that about your parents and sister as well?" It wasn't Vivien's nature to be coy, and she stopped it the moment she realized what she was doing. "One of the others might get the wrong idea about us."

"No, only the idea that I like you and have therefore spoken considerably to you. That's not wrong."

"I'm sure that at least one of the members of this party probably thinks that we tolerate each other more than we do."

"No. At least not on my part. And not a matter of toleration."

"You must then be playing the gallant gentleman, as is approved of in London."

"I'm only doing some of that. Being accurate, too, Miss Vivien. Precise and detached."

Because of her momentary instability, Vivien gave in to one particular feeling and said irritably, "I wish that you would speak in sentences with subjects and predicates, as so many people do."

"Excuse it." Arthur felt sure that the tips of his ears had reddened. "Miserable habit. Quite so."

She put a hand up over her lips to hide a smile at the clipped phrases in which he apologized for speaking in clipped phrases.

He said quickly, "I mean to say that it is a fault which many people deplore."

She grinned at his sudden carefulness, and he couldn't help smiling back.

"What I meant to convey, Mr. Fairfield, at the beginning of this stroll is that we have met only a while ago and it seems forward of you to be occupied only with me."

"Forward but right. Not excessively so. I mean to say, to point out, Miss Vivien, that—"

"I understand the burden of your song, Mr. Fairfield, so to speak." She felt that she was in control of her feelings but wildly emotional at the same time, which was palpably impossible. "You cannot escape the conclusion that it is not too soon in our acquaintance for you to be so carried away."

"It is possible to meet a girl and know from the minute that you want to be with her in the future. It must be possible. I can tell you this in an authoritative and truthful manner."

"Do you mean because it has happened to you so many times in the past?" She wasn't being coy again, but the speculation seriously occurred to her.

"Nothing whatever like this, Miss Vivien, has ever happened to me before."

His voice carried conviction. Without directly admitting her own sudden feelings towards him, Vivien found herself searching for objections to their further acquaintance.

"I am not invariably of an angelic temperament."

"Most human beings aren't."

"I have always lived in the country and am unused to London."

"Society in *le monde* will take to you immediately," he said with unquestioning warmth.

"Perhaps I could arrange a visit in the company of my Aunt Malbot so as to test the waters."

"You must do that, yes! It will be marvelous!"

"We can afford to know each other to a greater extent than we do now." She had almost conceded the attraction on her side and felt sure he understood. "For instance, I have no idea what you do."

"Oh, the usual. Clubs and balls and an occasional drink, and once in a while a sporting chance at the tables. Almack's is splendid for such purposes, though not what it was, I understand."

"I meant to ask about what you do for a living. What socially useful work keeps you busy, Mr. Fairfield?"

"Work? A position?"

Arthur's voice seemed briefly strangled. Too late it was occurring to him that a marvelous girl like Vivien wouldn't be able to accept any male unless he was a respectable member of society. Arthur was a gambler, a conscientious drinker, a hard-living celebrant, a splendid weekend guest. These attributes didn't qualify him as a husband and father. Not, certainly, in darling Vivien's eyes.

"A position. Yes, of course." It amazed him that words could issue forth from between his lips even if none possessed the slightest importance. "In the City, you know, I have a position in the City."

She accepted his statement that he was a cog in London's financial community, following, as everyone did, what was meant by his vague-sounding words.

"I'm sure I couldn't begin to understand everything involved by such efforts," she said sincerely, not aware that he had turned his head so she wouldn't see him looking thankful for her lack of knowledge. "But sometime in London you can try explaining it to me."

"Oh yes, certainly."

"Better yet, you can show me as much as you think a woman can comprehend about your role in those matters."

"Show you? Of course, yes. Absolutely." He drew himself

up, and only his close friends would have realized that he was in distress. "It will be an honor, Miss Vivien. Truly an honor."

The promenade came to its conclusion, and Arthur and Vivien joined the others in returning to the house. Mrs. Malbot was soon saying that dear Vivien was indisposed and not able to entertain upon the pianoforte, as she had fully intended to do. Anyone looking in Vivien's direction could see that she was speaking vivaciously with Arthur and had eyes and ears for no one else on earth.

It was a pensive Arthur, however, who demolished a solitary breakfast at seven-thirty on Saturday morning. He had slept raggedly. He was blinking at a great rate, befitting a young man who had previously considered the morning only as the proper time to get back home from a rout. His lounging coat and plaid trousers were probably being worn for the first time.

There was a look on his features that didn't have anything to do with *après* dissipation. Arthur resembled someone who stands before the gates of paradise and has just become aware that he had forgotten to bring a letter of introduction.

Because he glanced out at the morning light with some detachment, he discovered his younger sister on the grounds. Camilla stood disconsolately between the goat cart and one of the innumerable flowering urns. After swallowing the last of his weak bohea as if the stuff had been lapsang souchong, he charged into the open air, took a deep breath of that hideous stuff, and advanced upon his sister. As usual, he took no further notice of her saddened appearance. He spoke without a formal greeting.

"I'm in love."

"Splendid," Camilla said automatically, her private thoughts courteously put to one side. His previous autocratic tone in discussing her own possible future made it hard to resist some levity. "There is a quality about the Dowager Duchess of Strafford which must cause every male heart to pound a little faster."

He didn't rise to the bait. "I must speak to Mrs. Malbot, of course, and offer for Vivien. Vivien is so beautiful, so witty and warm and intelligent."

"You could do far worse," his sister said in a judicious spirit. "Let us prayerfully hope that your suit will be accepted."

"But there is a problem, Cammie." He was briefly wringing his hands. "You must advise me about what is to be done. I shall be brief. Purely to gain Vivien's interest and admiration, I permitted her to think that I am employed in London, in the City."

Camilla closed her eyes tightly. The thought of her brother unleashed in financial circles caused some pain. "If Vivien believes that, she must be in love."

"She expressed warmth, as, of course, a girl does at any fellow's conversation. And the long and the short of it, Cammie, is that Vivien hopes to see me at work during the time when she is in London."

"You can put her off. Tell her that a crisis impends in the purlieus of the financial community. Surely you can shade the truth with great deftness."

"Once, certainly. Not, if it comes to that, forever."

"Do you have any close friend who is employed in the City and could let you pretend for a day that you are of some use in the world?"

"Of course it can be done for a day, but if Vivien and I are to marry, it must be for longer and no masquerade can be allowed."

"Do I understand," Camilla asked, awed in spite of herself by this tangible proof of the much-vaunted power of a good woman's love, "that you are proposing to change your spots, unlike the proverbial leopard?"

"Cammie, I have to."

He was in anguish, and humor had become justly unwelcome. Camilla proceeded to give earnest thought to the difficulty.

"Could Trevor be useful if you take him into your confidence?"

"The Duke? Whom does he know in London unless one of us introduced him?"

"Perhaps our esteemed father can be of help."

"He is a diplomatist. Not acquainted in the financial community. The guv'nor would only make sympathetic noises but offer no real assistance. He never does."

It was a truth that Camilla declined to acknowledge, as ever, and she waved it away. At the same time she refrained from saying that Arthur was now in a garden, the prescribed place in which to eat worms.

"I see only a single solution," Camilla said thoughtfully. "When we return to London you are going to have to seek employment. Do it yourself, and not as someone asking for a favor but as a man willing to put the resources of his intellect into laboring for a worthy firm. Apply yourself, and you should get the results you want."

To this he agreed after a long pause. Without further conversation he turned on a heel and left.

Camilla, alone at last, resumed considering her own problem. It was necessary to face the need for telling Trevor that she felt their masquerade had to end gracefully. Too many relatives had been building expectations for them upon a foundation of sand. It was a prodigious unkindness that the two of them had committed, and she was angry at herself for not having realized it before agreeing to what had seemed like a pleasant lark.

With the need faced and admitted, she squared her shoulders and awaited a chance to lay down her ukase to Trevor.

CHAPTER TEN

It was close to twelve o'clock before Trevor alighted from a black Morvi two-wheeler carriage. Despite a white cloth cap, his even features showed a bit more of the sun's touch than before. Perhaps he had been kept busy in the outdoors by several of his farmer tenants. At sight of Camilla his nile green eyes glistened appreciatively.

"Ah, Miss Camilla." He deepened his voice as her present attitude became apparent. "You seem restless."

"That is one way to think about it, yes," she admitted judiciously.

"No doubt you crave some distraction," he concluded, not being entirely accurate. "I would assume that you aren't a horsewoman."

She was taken aback at what appeared to be a change of subject. "Absolutely not."

"Then you've rarely had the pleasure of riding."

"Not since very early childhood, when I was put on a small horse so as to amuse my family." She couldn't avoid shaking her head disapprovingly at the recollection. "But all this is by the way."

"I don't consider it so, Miss Camilla. Please allow me to compensate you for my morning's absence by showing you what a great pleasure you have been missing for these few years."

"I am hardly dressed for riding."

"You will be most comfortable, I can assure you, and will look typically splendid."

She was purposely wearing one of her favorite daytime rig-outs, pale yellow with sleeves fitted closely at the wrists. A poke bonnet helped display her candid blue eyes to best ef-fect, and her dark shoes were of the ankle-length, button-up variety which London girls currently favored for the prov-inces. Encased in this flattering concoction of effects, she would inform Trevor of the near-suspension of civilities upon which she had decided.

"I am determined that we confer as soon as may be."

"I have been conferring with others all morning, and will appreciate a further *pourparler* on horseback."

He was already in motion, a state which kept him from being observant or reasonably receptive. It was a quirk that she'd had occasion to discover at Ascot. If she wanted to unburden her mind it would be necessary to follow where he led.

The stables were located some two hundred feet from the rear of the house. The stableman, a burly man with huge hands, reminded her of those horsebreakers who crowded Piccadilly in the mornings, training their four-year-olds from the high box seats of their skeleton-breaks, which simulated carriages. A horse not much older than four was brought out for her, a dark brown animal which caused her to think that its color didn't go well with her clothing. She spurned assistance in mounting sidesaddle, but several false starts were made before she accomplished the task. That difficulty turned an irritation into a challenge, and she became determined to give a good account of herself on horseback.

The stableman advised gently, "You maun 'old the reins, miss."

Trevor added, "Keep them in your left hand. Push the left rein against his neck, say, and he'll move as you indicate."

Trevor was already approaching a chestnut which waited impatiently for him. He mounted with skill, one leg extended, and sat stiff-backed with his weight balanced.

Camilla found herself pleased that she was on a level with him and sensed that her horse was gentle and affectionate. She touched the back of its neck with her palm.

Trevor said, "First you walk, Miss Camilla, and then you trot. As Ginger, your horse, trots, you rise with him."

His own animal was already moving forward. From over a shoulder Trevor issued what was almost certainly a compliment to any equestrienne. "You have a beautiful seat on a horse."

Had he looked around at that point, he would have seen Miss Camilla Fairfield flush to the roots of her blond hair.

Ginger began to walk. Camilla found the sensation pleasant after the first inevitable moment of fright. Trevor's mount was already cantering, and he sat with his arms pulled against his body without looking back. Camilla wanted to ride as Trevor was doing, but knew she would find it beyond her present capacities.

Some unwitting gesture of hers must have constricted the reins just as the horse had started to walk. Ginger now began cantering. Camilla rose slightly when the animal had two legs in the air. At the first shock of adjusting to Ginger's rhythm, she called out.

Trevor looked back as the sound left Camilla's lips. He turned his animal in her direction. Enviously she saw that he and the horse moved with ease.

"Are you well?"

"Thank you." She was in no 'mood to speak about her momentary discomfort.

"I hope that you are enjoying Ginger's company."

"Yes." And when she gave it a moment's thought, the answer seemed correct. Moving through the air in this mode was bracing, although she remained keenly aware of her own shortcomings and of the animal's tolerance for them. "I like it very much indeed."

"Ah, I knew that an upbringing in London would not have entirely spoiled *your* sensibilities, if I might say so." He grinned. "My suggestion would be that you hold the reins a little more loosely if only to help Ginger become accustomed to your style."

She appreciated the tactful choice of words.

"Just before, you said something about a conference or a

discussion," he added thoughtfully. "Could the matter wait till we have concluded our ride?"

Camilla agreed, not wanting to spoil the impromptu excursion either.

There was nothing, however, of "our ride" about the jaunt they were taking. Trevor's mount pawed the ground on account of the relative freedom given him. At a stimulus so deftly applied that she couldn't identify it, the chestnut trotted away once again. As Camilla watched, unmoving, Trevor rode to a point where he seemed able to touch the horizon. For the first time during his most recent sortie, he looked back. At sight of Camilla having stayed far behind, he turned his horse around and started back to offer help.

Seeing him come closer, she greeted him by raising a hand. It was an error. As she wasn't standing, the motion caused some elevation in one foot. Ginger promptly interpreted this as a signal to trot.

Scorning the walk or canter which were only preliminary exercises, Ginger fairly flew. Camilla felt that she had already moved part of her body too effectively and tried to be as still as the circumstances would allow. It was fear that dictated her position, not the balanced weight used by a capable rider. Ginger, an amiable but unforgiving beast, was well aware of her weakness. She was being brought closer to Trevor, which was a comfort. No doubt he quickly saw what was happening.

"Pull the reins gently," he called.

She was unable to comply. Moisture on her hands, brought on by uncertainty, caused her to attempt the motion in vain. The reins slipped through her hands. She had lost all control.

Ginger, feeling free as the air itself, rode down the path, headed, perhaps, for the horizon itself.

Trevor had sensed what was happening, however, a moment before the horse started its dash. Spurring his own steed to follow, he reached out for the reins. He missed by inches. Camilla held onto what she thought of as the doorknob of the saddle, but only one hand could be accommodated. Trying to add her right hand to the fixture and give herself greater purchase, she lost her balance. Even as she fell, she appreciated that Trevor had alertly pulled himself and his mount out of the way, avoiding what could have been a greater accident.

She dropped to her left side. The path was blessedly soft. She stayed motionless, giving silent thanks for her deliverance. At the same time she was making up her mind that in another encounter with the benighted Ginger, results would be different.

"Camilla! Camilla!" It was Trevor, all the courtesies of their usual discourse generally forgotten. "Are you all right."

"Yes."

"Are you sure of that?"

After a pause she said, in a slightly different tone, "This is not an easy position in which to hold a dialogue."

He was impervious to even the mildest sarcasm. "Stretch yourself a little and let me know immediately if you feel the slightest pain."

"You shall be the first to be taken into my confidence . . . no pain. None whatever."

"The fingers? The toes?"

"Nowhere."

"Thank heavens." She could see his relieved features framed by the cloudless June sky. He might have been some angel descended to save her.

"Please sit up slowly. Very good. Now I ask you to hold out your hands. I will grip them."

His hands were firm and blessedly strong.

"Now I am going to raise you to your feet."

He suited his action to the words. She was aware of being gently but determinedly raised, then pulled towards him. A riot of colors formed in her eyes as she moved. It was clear, too, that dirt was caked on what had once been pale yellow clothes, but she didn't feel the least concern about it.

She was on her feet now. His hands loosened, then suddenly gripped with even more tightness.

"Oh, Camilla, Camilla," said the Duke of Strafford in a husky voice, "I am so happy that you are unhurt."

She found herself stirred by his palpable goodwill. His closeness while she had been incapacitated hadn't seemed forward of him, but he wasn't moving away now. Indeed, his face was coming yet closer. His lips found hers. It was a kiss impelled by gratitude at her fortune but ignited by happiness. She never remembered if she gave him the slightest assistance.

A hint of June breeze must have reminded both of them that they were involved with private familiarities upon a bridal path.

He pulled away, his cheeks reddening. "I beg your pardon, Cam—Miss Camilla. I most humbly beg your pardon."

It was on the tip of her tongue to say that there was no need. She didn't speak, remembering that it was incumbent upon her to tell Trevor very shortly that they could no longer see each other on the basis that had so clearly made both of them contented.

"I do apologize for having taken advantage of your being upset," he added softly. Before any disclaimer might be ventured, he asked, "Are you able to walk?"

"Not quite as well as usual," she said after brief experimentation.

She would have welcomed a strong hand on hers to help keep her upright. Trevor didn't move until he was sure she could walk by herself. With his right hand he then reached for his horse's reins and led it behind them. Camilla told herself that the horse needed Trevor's guidance more than she did. If she had been in the mood to feel amused, she would have laughed.

As they neared the stable, he called out. The burly stableman rushed to his side, listened briefly, then mounted Trevor's horse and rode off in search of the errant Ginger.

"That fool of a four-year-old will ride up to the knacker's one day," Trevor grumbled. "I don't doubt there'll be a roaring welcome for him."

Carefully she walked at his side to the rear of the house. Trevor called for a maid and asked her to send Annie outside posthaste.

It was hardly any sooner said than done. The Fairfields' invaluable maid ran out, gave one look, and reached for her

young mistress around the midriff. It was in vain for Camilla
to say that such ministrations were unnecessary. As a loyal
servant Annie knew no reason for accepting instructions during what was perceived as an emergency.

"What 'appened?" Annie demanded as she needlessly led
Camilla past the stained-glass horror and up the stairs.

"I fell from a horse."

" 'Osses is dangerous," Annie said firmly. "I used to walk
out with a gentleman as was a groom at the Newmarket races,
and 'e could tell the most 'ideous stories about 'osses, 'e
could."

"I plan to see for myself if horses are a danger to any
sensible and careful rider."

"What? After an 'orrible fall, you'd go out on one 'a those
monsters again?"

"Until the accident took place, I was enjoying myself considerably."

In her dismay Annie let Camilla go. As a result Camilla was
able to walk swiftly into her guest room and shut the door on
herself. At her first sight of this refuge yesterday, she could
have used Annie's assistance. There was a barricade of
painted windows not sufficiently hidden by painted curtains.
Nature scenes defaced the floorcloth and the wallpaper, with
its coordinated borders that always made Camilla blink if she
gave them the least attention. She was grateful that nature
scenes hadn't been painted on the Chippendale chairs, but
wouldn't have been surprised to look under the huge bed and
discern an image of varicolored and sickly looking birds wal-
lowing in sunshine. The decorator of this room, having hit
upon a good idea, had been unable to relinquish it.

Hardly had she changed into a royal blue, which had been
handed down by her older sister before marriage, when Lady
Fairfield came rushing in.

"That rig-out doesn't become you and you should never
have brought it along," Mamma said promptly, and then reminded herself of Annie's communication, which had
brought her to these precincts. "Are you sure that you remain
unhurt after your fall?"

"Quite sure."

"Even so, I wish you wouldn't race around the room like a gazelle."

"I am not moving at a greater speed than usual," Camilla said patiently.

"At least you have to divest yourself of that eyesore rig-out and stay here long enough for dear Trevor to feel some concern about your welfare."

Camilla refrained from pointing out that it was similar wisdom which had caused her to accept Trevor's plan to counterfeit strong feelings in the first place.

"I am sure that your father will want to confirm that you are not harmed," Mamma said. "Wait here."

Lady Fairfield made her departure, leaving the door wide open, perhaps so that she could observe whether Camilla shortly made a dash to freedom.

There was a sudden bickering chorus of rising sounds in the hallway and she heard the raised voice of Lady Fairfield in counterpoint to the soothing tones of Sir Osric and the offended arpeggios of Mrs. Malbot. The latter's idea of discourse apparently consisted of taking offense first and apologizing gracefully after a passage of time.

No apologies would be forthcoming on this occasion. It was possible to hear an occasional sentence fragment amid the hubbub.

". . . I will not allow my niece to accept . . ."

"My son is far too young and inexperienced . . ."

At Sir Osric's hushed urging, hostilities were adjourned to one of the chambers. Camilla had heard enough to gain the clear impression that her brother had recently spoken to Mrs. Malbot in offering for Vivien. Presumably that gorgon had sought out Arthur's parents, and the lively discussion followed. Camilla hoped that Arthur and Vivien would find happiness together in spite of family objections on both sides.

At a time like this it was possible for her to leave the house unobserved by either distracted parent, as she had already decided upon doing. In the course of making an egress, she was fortunate enough to avoid the presence of her brother as well. Nor did she see Trevor. At this time she didn't want to see or think about His Grace, the Duke of Strafford.

The burly stableman objected to her plans for taking out the recently returned Ginger. Camilla, however, wouldn't be swayed. For one thing, he was not virtually a family member like the hardworking Annie and could therefore be overruled with impunity. She did soothe his feelings by listening keenly to the instructions he offered and asking questions to aid her understanding of maneuvers to be successfully followed on what she declined to think of as the bridal path.

She showed herself a good student from her perch atop the still energetic Ginger. A delightful half hour on horseback followed. She rested, then spent more time with that forgiving beast, who recognized authority when he encountered it.

Returning to the house at last, Camilla felt fresh and invigorated at having proved her worth as a participant in what she had finally realized was a delightful and rewarding sport. In her current euphoric state she accepted the thought equably that a difficult evening lay directly ahead.

CHAPTER ELEVEN

It was her plan to discuss matters with Trevor before supper began. To accomplish that worthy goal she changed quickly into the white, with its becomingly low bodice and the dark lace front, then hurried down to the overfurnished large sitting room. Here she discovered the considerate host awaiting his and his mother's guests.

"May I speak with you?"

"Certainly," Trevor said, well aware that she wanted comparative privacy. "Will you take a turn about the room with me?"

She silently applauded his good sense, knowing that it would be possible to modulate her voice along the route and not be heard by later arrivals. Afterwards he was likely to consider her words over the repast, while probably studying her in extremely becoming white, with that low bodice dropping to just above the waist.

"I understand that you had a triumph with Ginger a while ago," he said approvingly as she put her hand on the back of his.

The first interruption came as their walk was getting under way. Mamma entered, bickering with Mrs. Malbot. Sir Osric had apparently chosen to dissociate himself from the difficulty at this time. The loyal Camilla couldn't blame him.

Vivien, coming in behind her aunt, looked pained. She glanced around swiftly, hoping to find Arthur. At sight of Camilla she nodded awkwardly. Upon receiving a warm smile in return, her eyes brightened. At another time, as both girls must have known, Camilla would have run to embrace Vivien and refer to her delightedly as sister.

"Most unsuitable at this time," Mamma was saying frigidly. "My boy is far too young for any serious consideration of lifelong engagements."

Mrs. Malbot's icily angry features gave her the appearance, in Camilla's eyes, of a crazed Dresden shepherdess. "I have been assured by the gossip newspapers from London that Arthur Fairfield is a womanizer and a gambler. You cannot expect me to approve the union of my niece with such a man."

"I do not seek your approval but a retraction of such ill-considered statements."

Vivien showed no inclination to leave the scene of battle, a trait which Camilla silently applauded. She wasn't one of those overbred London girls determined to be terribly lady-like but fully prepared to commit murder only from behind a victim's back. She glared at both older women, attempting to wither each in full oratorical flight. It was useless, of course.

Trevor turned to Camilla, wordless but clearly far from amused. Here was another justification for his cynical attitude about the search for wedded bliss. Camilla knew that it wasn't the proper time to discuss her newly aroused feelings against the scheme on which the two of them had embarked. Only after a pause would she be able to commence that particular fray.

Into this scene Sir Osric brought a subdued Arthur. Vivien turned to him. From that moment neither seemed prepared to acknowledge that anyone else was in the room. Camilla sensed that Trevor had noticed this byplay, as he noticed so much else. She wondered if, like herself, he wasn't at least somewhat envious.

Sir Osric, behaving as if everything was serenely normal, murmured to his host, "This country air of yours works up a most enormous appetite in me."

It was left to the Dowager Duchess to force some cessation of hostilities between the older women. Last to arrive and looking particularly well in turquoise and white that had been cut for the London of ten years ago, she instantly understood what was happening and addressed both combatants impartially.

"It seems only proper to rest the humors before and during supper," she said. "Indeed, I take advantage of the rights of a hostess to insist upon your doing so."

Mamma, to her credit, was the first to concede the point. Looking as if she had swallowed a rabbit in one gulp, she forced a smile.

"Let us postpone any discussion of these matters," Mrs. Malbot said, ever ready to made amends no matter how furious she had become.

"Certainly," said Mamma, determined not to be outdone. "I have been most unfair."

"No more than I," Mrs. Malbot said. "Not one whit more than I."

Trevor intervened in time to prevent the start of another likely quarrel about which of the two women had been behaving more regrettably.

It was no surprise that conversation languished over the excellent supper. Lady Fairfield and Mrs. Malbot measured each other during the turtle soup, each perhaps thinking that the other's features rather resembled the cutlets soubise set before them, although Mrs. Malbot had the *élan vital* of the larded guinea fowl which followed. No hint of good feeling returned over the flanc meringue or the sizzling oolong tea.

Such conversation as took place was traded charily by the host and his mother, with Camilla joining to an even greater extent than Sir Osric. She had seen Sir Osric being at ease over a meal at home that interrupted some domestic disagreement, while Mamma, in turn, was too sweet for words. Tonight, though, each seemed preoccupied.

Supper was followed by the usual stroll about the grounds, Trevor walking with Camilla but keeping himself not far from the recent combatants. Unlike Sir Osric, who looked bemused, Trevor was prepared to enforce tranquility, mostly for his mother's sake. Once again Camilla was unable to speak to him privately. She didn't feel as uncomfortable as Arthur and

Vivien, though, forced to walk alongside their relatives yet
turning to look at each other all the time. Little wonder that
Sir Osric was bemused while Lady Fairfield walked rigidly and
Mrs. Malbot sounded like that kettle over which the oolong
tea had been prepared and later served.

Back at the large sitting, with coats and mantles cast off,
Trevor said amiably that he looked forward to hearing Miss
Camilla sing.

"My voice is ill equipped for vocalizing tonight," she said
promptly and truthfully.

Lady Fairfield looked displeased but contained herself. Sir
Osric seemed approving. Trevor and the Dowager Duchess
appeared politely regretful. Mrs. Malbot looked sullen,
though relieved that no straw had broken this camel's back.
Arthur and Vivien, as before, had eyes only for each other and
couldn't have told anyone what was taking place in their vicinity.

"Perhaps a little gaming would be suitable," the Dowager
Duchess suggested. "It would rest us all from the most di-
verse worries."

Unfortunately, the Dowager Duchess played whist above all
other games, and it would have been impossible to exclude
her. Only four players could be occupied at each table. She
and Trevor sat down to game with Sir Osric and Camilla. It
suddenly occurred to Camilla that the arrangement would
leave both older women inactive and glaring at the besotted
niece and son.

Trevor, who had seen Camilla look warily from one woman
to the other, suddenly made apologies for his inability to play
at this time.

Mrs. Malbot was lured into the game. She shuffled the cards
awkwardly, dropping half a dozen, then cut brusquely and
dealt as if she couldn't wait to force the pasteboards away
from her.

Camilla had been unable to speak with Trevor during the
balance of the night's entertainment. On Sunday morning she
woke early. Trevor had not done likewise, as she saw at break-

fast. She attempted to beguile time by renewing her acquaintance with Ginger. Suggs, the heavy stableman, forcefully pointed out that nobody did any riding for pleasure on Sunday morning.

A council of males decided that the Fairfield wagonette must be employed for the trip to church, the day's primary activity. On board was stowed the host and his mother, along with the remaining guests. Camilla observed that Mamma and Mrs. Malbot took pains to be calm while on the way to commune with their Maker. Nor did anyone glare at Arthur and Vivien, smiling foolishly at each other.

The ritual of greeting neighbors and asking and answering minor questions occupied some small amount of time. In the course of those exchanges Camilla was able to speak briefly with Trevor.

"I hope that we will soon be able to have a longer discussion."

"Certainly," Trevor smiled. "Come to my study some ten minutes after we arrive back home."

He was obviously looking forward to being closeted with her. He enjoyed Camilla's company for its own sake, as she did his. Unfortunately there wouldn't be the least enjoyment in the meeting she had planned.

Nor was there much gratification from the sermon at St. Simon's-in-the-Fields. The Reverend Mr. Formond was one of those clerics who was determined to link spiritual matters with recent events, as if to prove that he was a sentient being. Today he deplored the relatively recent death of the Marquis of Wellesley, former Governor General of India, a man who Mr. Formond had once greeted briefly. The labor riots in the industrial north drew none of his sympathy, but warmth returned to his tones in discussing the Treaty of Nanking between Britain and China. He felt that it would be of help to the poor heathen of Hong Kong, of which Britain was now the owner.

The ride back to Strafford was a difficult one, Mamma and Mrs. Malbot glaring at each other now that they had communed with their Maker and He was presumably looking the other way. Only Arthur and Vivien were unaffected by the women's attitudes.

In her room Camilla changed her deep azure travel turnout of muslin, which was sufficiently attractive for that purpose but not at all what she had imagined herself wearing when she faced Trevor. She did rub at her cheeks with paper to give them a needed glow. Her appearance seemed satisfactory but not dazzling.

Trevor welcomed her to the large and airy room with a desk and more types of chairs than she had felt were possible. In his waistcoat, cut high at the neck, and his tight trousers he was a dashing figure.

"Is something wrong?" he asked as she settled herself at last and he sat opposite her.

"Yes." She had to look down at herself as she spoke. "I am afraid that we have gone too far."

"Do you feel that one kiss, administered as a restorative measure when you seemed *in extremis,* amounts to illicit passion?"

She flushed at hearing the last term, but it did impel her to look up directly at him and show herself as being calm. "Not at all. I mean that we have gone too far in pretending."

"We have pretended only to a certain depth of feeling for each other, and that in order to save ourselves from many nuisances of which we are both aware."

"As a result, however, your mother seriously considers the prospect of impending nuptials, which won't happen. She can hardly help but be unsettled by the circumstance. You may well imagine that my own mother has been in transports of happiness, which are entirely justified."

"Older women are indeed emotional, as we all have reason to know after this weekend." He shuddered lightly, recollecting Lady Fairfield and Mrs. Malbot's verbal jousts.

"The difficulty is that our behavior builds up hope in others," she pointed out, making herself unmistakably clear. "These others do have a stake in what happens to us."

Trevor's face whitened. He had surely spoken to his mother and been aware of the expectant faces of others around him.

Most likely he hadn't considered the effects of his actions until Camilla's words forced him to do so.

"It is a game that must stop," she added quietly.

"Very well." He spread both hands as if to say more. "I—I shall miss you as a companion."

It had crossed her mind that he might perhaps want to retain the pleasure of her company and draw closer as a result. The idea had been mistaken.

She rose, prepared to turn and leave.

"We can surely talk to each other at social gatherings." He was smiling now, putting the best face on her rejection of facile compromise. "Briefly, of course."

Camilla was unable to respond with the amusement she partly felt at his continued wish to dissemble in front of sharp-eyed matchmakers. Her feelings were not soothed at all by sharing his impulse. It would be thoughtless to others, as she had realized, if she gave in.

"Perhaps," he suggested—and she wondered if the lightness in his voice was feigned—"a nod could be offered without offense taken by the other party. I think that we might reach an understanding about smiles."

She turned abruptly towards the opened door and walked out of the room. Only a few minutes had been required for him to lose his sympathetic warmth, to lose access to the humor they shared and the ease that they had known together. Not since childhood had she been given to thinking of herself as being in love, but when the concept came to her on the way out of this house her mind didn't reject it.

CHAPTER TWELVE

Preparations for departure were concluded at last. Haircloth trunks had been packed by Annie at a furious rate, deposited in the prescribed space above the wagonette, and then tied down. The Cleveland Bays had been affixed, as Sir Osric evasively called the process, to the carriage front. The Fairfield coachmen, in newly purchased dark greatcoats that wouldn't show dirt so quickly and cost the earth because of that, were rising in place on the vehicle.

Camilla emerged just as the work-worn Annie was taking what must have been her first deep breath since arriving in the peaceful countryside.

Mamma, looking genially at her, said, "I certainly think you would have gained a few stone in weight from a relaxing weekend such as this."

Annie rolled her eyes to heaven, but only briefly. She was a well-trained servant with many years of experience.

"You're one of those fortunate people who never gain weight no matter how much they eat or rest," Lady Fairfield said enviously. "How I wish I was that way myself!"

Some fifty feet off was a two-wheeled gig with a single coachman. In this smaller contrivance Mrs. Malbot and her niece would soon be leaving. Lady Fairfield avoided looking in that direction, and Mrs. Malbot returned the dubious compliment.

The Dowager Duchess of Strafford, who had made farewells to her guests only a while ago, emerged from the house to continue her efforts. She found herself moving from the wagonette to the gig as Mrs. Malbot and Lady Fairfield declined to come close to one another.

"So pleasant that you could be with us," she murmured several times. She had already made apologies for Trevor's absence, claiming that he had been called away suddenly by one of his farmers.

Camilla was aware of the Dowager Duchess eyeing her while that explanation was offered to the Fairfields. No doubt Trevor had just spoken to her about his actual position *vis-à-vis* the comely Miss Fairfield. The Dowager Duchess now knew about the conspiracy and the reasons for its having been shattered.

Lady Fairfield, having left the issuing of compliments to her verbally adroit spouse, suddenly asked, "Where is that son of ours?"

"Arthur will emerge shortly, I feel confident."

"You had best go back and root him out." Lady Fairfield looked at Sir Osric being confronted by the prospect of a family mission. "Never mind! I will do it. As always."

Arthur himself emerged in moments. He walked slowly, blinking in the June sunlight. His ever-pale skin seemed to have developed folds overnight. When he saw Vivien, however, he straightened and color appeared in the suddenly smoothed cheeks. No longer was he prematurely aged.

Vivien's eyes found him at the same time, and she rushed in his direction. They were kissing in public, doing it with a fervor that must have reminded the middle-aged witnesses of their youth. Camilla, also watching, felt pleased for the couple and wished there was a certain man with whom she could share happiness.

Mrs. Malbot suddenly cleared her throat. Vivien drew her lips reluctantly from Arthur's.

"We will meet in London," she said clearly, and Camilla didn't doubt it any more than did the other unwilling listeners. "My Aunt Malbot and I will visit as soon as I hear from you accordingly, and see that you are indeed a fine and up-standing and useful member of society."

Arthur, who couldn't possibly blanch—and certainly not

while under the eyes of the girl he loved—came close to accomplishing the feat.

This time he lowered his lips to Vivien's. Their kiss was brief. He drew away regretfully. He might have been a gallant soldier kissing his love good-bye shortly before going into battle.

Slowly he walked to the carriage, so miserable that he didn't see his mother look at Vivien and then turn towards her son again. The look on Lady Fairfield's face was of sorrow mixed with understanding, and didn't resemble any that her daughter had ever encountered on that terrain. Camilla supposed that when her own marriage was announced, Mamma would be happy for her; but accepting the thought of her only son most likely leaving the family home in a short while was a task that she could perform only with deliberation and some pain.

Camilla had dreaded the forthcoming trip, if only because it would certainly be marred by Mamma asking about His Grace and planning the nuptials, which weren't going to occur, with the groom she visualized for her remaining daughter.

In these forebodings, however, Camilla had been mistaken. Mamma sat quietly throughout the journey from the interior, looking at her son and not saying a word. Arthur was quiet as well. Only his sister recognized the hangdog expression on his face.

Sir Osric, seeing that his son was unresponsive to any discussion, expended some of his erudition about Kent in a monologue addressed to his daughter. When they passed orchards with apples and later with cherries, he told Camilla that in both cases the original seeds had been imported from Flanders into the Britain ruled by Henry the Eighth. Upon riding past areas devoted to the raising of wheat and oats, to barley for malting, to potatoes, Sir Osric dipped further into his store of facts. The sight of sheep brought out the longest entries from his catalog of knowledge about the area.

Camilla smiled or nodded and spoke briefly when some acknowledgment was needed. About the majestic oaks and the beech woods Sir Osric knew little or nothing, and from these bulwarks of nature Camilla drew the most enjoyment.

It was a relieved young woman who returned to London with her family by evening. It had been a stirring visit for Arthur as well as herself. She felt pleased for her brother and certain that his dilemma would be solved in a few days. At the same time she would have been less than a human being if part of her didn't wish that the entire visit had never taken place.

At the house in Lower Brook Street everything was substantially as it had been left. Determining that much, beyond question, needed Mamma's unremitting toil for the next hour and a half. Camilla was only too glad to fall into a dreamless sleep, which she did at ten-thirty.

The morning was occupied by making sure that the wagonette would be returned in good condition to the ever-irascible Sir Victor. Mamma was confidently able to predict that the wealthy portrait painter would create many causes for complaint at the condition of the vehicle. As it turned out, she underestimated Sir Victor's capacity to find nonexistent difficulties.

Camilla retired to the small sitting room upstairs and the needlepoint that awaited her. She hoped that Mamma would not contemplate inquiring after her whereabouts until considerable time had passed. During the interim it might be possible to decide exactly what to say when Mamma asked about the state of what was supposed to be her budding romance with the redoubtable Trevor. As it happened, Mamma entered the room not long afterwards.

"We have hardly spoken for a while," Mamma began, choosing words which augured badly for Camilla's serenity. Mamma's first thoughts, however, as might have been expected, were on another. "You probably know that Arthur has to find some dreary position if he wants to marry that girl what's-her-name."

Camilla decided against supplying a name that Mamma not only knew but would never forget. Mamma's aggrieved tones, as if some hideous injustice was being perpetrated, did require some correction.

"I fail to see that respectable employment is more degrading than constant carousals."

"Your brother never—well, rarely." Lady Fairfield looked away at sight of the incipient smile on Camilla's lips. "He is a male, after all, and it is necessary that a male sow his wild oats."

"I am sure he has a crop that Kent itself wouldn't hold by this time."

"That is no way to speak of your brother," Lady Fairfield said mechanically. She seemed too weary for her usual dogmatic defense of Arthur. "He will certainly arrange matters very soon if that's what he wishes. Your brother can be most competent."

Camilla hoped that Mamma was in the right of that. She made the error of saying so.

"I hope that you, Cammie, will attain your heart's desire as well as your brother is going to," Lady Fairfield said, made vigorous by a second expression of doubt concerning her son. "I am reminded to ask about your dealings with dear Trevor. He chose not to bid the assembled guests a farewell."

"I understood that he was called away by a farmer on the land."

"But he did not say adieu to anyone before it was necessary for him to leave." Lady Fairfield looked shrewdly at her younger daughter, eyes squinted in an unbecoming fashion for once. "Was he unable to face you again? Had there been a quarrel?"

Sooner or later, this nettle would have to be grasped.

"Indeed there had."

"And what was the subject of the disagreement?"

Camilla knew that in time it would be necessary to explain everything that had taken place and the reasons for it. If nothing else, a baring of the facts would keep Mamma from thinking of the Duke as a prospective son-in-law.

Lady Fairfield was not in the mood to permit silence. "Young woman, I trust that you are not going to destroy a

splendid chance for an early marriage." Judicial thought com-
pelled her to add, "My marriage to your father was a relatively
late one and has been successful, but the earlier in life that
one plunges into the maelstrom, so to speak, the greater are
one's chances for a successful accommodation and the pursu-
ant happiness."

It was a dubious proposition at best, when put in those
terms. Camilla was not disposed to play with words at this
particular time.

"I was afraid that the Duke wanted to hurt you and the
Dowager Duchess both." In part that was so. She hadn't realized the possible damage that might be done by his and her
own feckless conduct. When that truth was pointed out,
Trevor had remained so angry at the legions of demonic hus-
band-hunters that he wasn't inclined to make the required
change.

"Trevor wants to delay your marriage, I assume." Mamma
had leaped to the first obvious conclusion. "Some men do
that in hopes that they will obtain what they truly want from
an anxious girl. And then, as often as not, there is no marriage
after all. You were entirely in the right, Cammie dear."

She wasn't used to having Mamma take her part in any
quarrel involving her with another. Most likely it had happened because Lady Fairfield was not yet aware of all the facts.
Permitting her to believe what was untrue would avoid a
brouhaha, but it seemed proper to practice honesty with someone who was giving thought to Camilla's interests.

While looking at a point to the right of Mamma's chair it
was easy to speak. The conspiracy was explained along with
her motives for destroying what had been a most pleasant
arrangement.

"You are now *au courant* of what has taken place," Camilla
said in conclusion.

"I see." It was impossible for even the most dutiful of
daughters to know what Mamma was feeling. For a woman
who rarely made a secret of her nerve storms, who discussed
them at the slightest inducement, who would probably have
orated at the Lords about the exasperatingly high prices she

encountered in buying porcelain miniatures at Fribourg & Treyer in the Haymarket, Lady Fairfield was extraordinarily restrained.

"I see," she said once more. "Is he—the Duke—is he a man you like?"

Camilla responded to the voice, which was not heightened by outrage or anger. "Trevor is not a thoughtless man save in this one area in which he feels he has been tormented beyond belief—and where I am most sympathetic. Otherwise he is not, as I say, in the least bit selfish."

"You show some feeling for him," Mamma decided. "Because it is not returned as fully as it is given, you must devote all your energies to seeking out another well-connected young man who is worthy of you."

Camilla's sudden astonishment caused her jaw to drop.

"Your brother should not be the only one of my children who will marry according to choice," Mamma added, perhaps optimistically. She had given considerable thought to the developments of the recent weekend, as well as Camilla's explanation. "I am now satisfied that you could capture the interest of a young man, even if the circumstances in that other case were somewhat *outré*. From which I infer that there must be a more serious contender for your hand somewhere in the offing. It is your task to find him. With, I may add, the most thoughtful help that a mother can offer."

It was clear that Camilla was no longer going to be thrust willy-nilly at any young male of a proper station.

Camilla and her mother suddenly stood at the same time, both with hands outstretched. The two females hugged each other and kissed, fervently on Camilla's part for the first time in several years. Never before had it crossed Camilla's mind that someday she and her mother could evolve in their feelings towards each other. After many autocratic demands on the part of one and rebellion from the other, the passage of time and increase of understanding from both was certain to bring them together into a state of (the concept was breathtaking) friendship.

CHAPTER THIRTEEN

A surprisingly brief supper had been completed on Monday evening before Camilla was informed of plans for the night. Sir Osric had purchased seats for the current *opérette* at the Theatre Royal in Drury Lane, and it was clear that everybody would be proceeding to that well-known temple of pleasure.

Camilla felt convinced that Arthur would once again classify himself as being indisposed. Apparently, though, her brother was so tired from his peregrinations around the City in search of elusive respectability that he acceded with weariness to Mamma's wishes.

Accordingly the family members paused only to repair such ravages as supper had inflicted on clothing and effects. The family carriage took them to Catherine Street in Covent Garden. More time than necessary was occupied in greeting acquaintances before entering. Camilla did not understand the reason for such an excess of joviality until Mamma suddenly shrugged and turned to Sir Osric.

"He won't be here," she said tiredly.

As if in silent apology, she glanced at her daughter.

Camilla asked quickly, "Was some young man expected?"

"We had hoped that Freddie Fawthorp would show himself," Mamma explained. "A splendid young man who has recently emigrated to London from somewhere in Sussex, I believe. Lady Darnborough has just told me that her nephew, Freddie of course, who generally accompanies her on such jaunts nowadays, has decided against doing so for once. He is fully occupied on business that has to do with a tunnel, I do believe."

Sir Osric supplied information as usual. "The Thames Tunnel between Rotherhithe and Wapping that Mr. Brunel is building."

Arthur, who had been absently hearing every fifth word, asked, "Do you suppose that Freddie Fawthorp can hire one more navvy for the work?"

"Arthur!" Lady Fairfield was shocked by her son's grim levity. "You hardly need to sink so low."

Camilla murmured, "Literally, in this case."

"Some excellent commercial opportunity will surely arise," Mamma continued, "if only you keep looking."

A despondent remark hovered on Arthur's lips, but it would only expose him to more in the way of automatic encouragement. He kept it to himself while acknowledging Camilla's hesitant smile.

The family proceeded inside. Here, as had been planned, they encountered Louise and her husband, the latter known to Camilla and Arthur as "Anthony the Rotter." This meeting had been planned earlier. Together, the females in animated conversation, they all dawdled to the well-appointed box for which Sir Osric had disgorged one pound two and six.

The entertainment was proceeding as the group disposed themselves on various plush seats. Mr. Frederick Balfe's musical gewgaw *The Bohemian Girl*, was once again being successfully performed, to judge from the audience's rapt silence. Love songs were a source of continuing irritation to Camilla, who fidgeted through them. Arthur sat with downcast eyes. Louise and Anthony, whose marriage was far from harmonious, were smiling amiably at one another. Mamma and Sir Osric were actually holding hands, which seemed to Camilla like an obscenity committed in public. But she saw the contentment in their propinquity, then smiled at her own momentary intolerance. Nevertheless she looked the other way.

In time there was a pause in the caterwauling, interspersed by speeches of love and loss that everyone but the speakers and singers knew would be temporary. Camilla and Arthur surged out to the rotunda, followed by sluggards. Arthur immersed himself in the duty of pretending to look at the familiar statues of Kean, Garrick, and an ill-at-ease Shakespeare who always seemed to Camilla as if he wanted to put both hands over his ears. The Fairfields chattered with Louise and her drunken dolt of a spouse. Camilla, impatient, proceeded to pace the area while carefully avoiding friends, acquaintances, and strangers who appeared deeply involved in unimportant conversations.

Her name was suddenly called out by a voice she had never heard before. It happened just as she was rounding the bust of Samuel Whitbread, that wealthy brewer who had raised money to rebuild the fire-racked Theatre Royal back in '08 or perhaps '09.

"You are Camilla Fairfield," this apparition asserted positively. "You were pointed out to me."

The stranger was female and not a day over twenty. Her blazing red hair was set in too many ringlets, and she had adorned them with a three-color muslin cap. Her dress seemed to consist more of tassels than cloth. Laced boots looked out of place, along with the rest of her rig-out. Instead of politely calling attention to its wearer, this girl's clothes and accessories simply howled for it.

"Is there something I can do for you?"

"There certainly is. What I want is for you to stop haunting my man."

"I beg your pardon?" Camilla had been feeling inured to surprises, but even the slightest acquaintance with this creature was apparently the antidote for indifference.

There was a signal that another outburst of music and prosiness would shortly be at hand from the stage. Camilla felt not the least hesitation in avoiding even a few minutes of Mr. Balfe's dramaturgy and clearing up the imputation against her corporeal self. She led the way over to the foot of the staircase towards the Grand Circle, an area which would be reasonably hushed.

"To be breathtakingly honest, you have somewhat the advantage of me. You know my name, to pick the clearest example, but I don't know yours."

"I'm Edith Jessop."

Camilla didn't intend to convey how little the intelligence meant, as it was a name she had never heard before. At sight of her expression, nevertheless, the other girl looked irritated.

"And when you say that I am haunting whoever it is you refer to as your man, Miss Jessop, I can assure you that I am not at this time aware of his identity."

"Oh, now, aren't you?" Edith Jessop stood with hand on hip, brows quirked disbelievingly. Her high voice was far from cultured.

It was this last manifestation which gave Camilla a jarring indication of who it was that might be meant.

"I hope that you will speak the man's name," she said.

"All right, I'll do even that if it helps in making everything plain as paint. It's Willie Royde, that's who my man is. Or was, until you came into his life." She made a fist. "Now he buys me tickets to performances like this, but won't come with me. I don't hardly see him from one day to the next. He talks about 'Lady Fortune,' that's how he calls you, and of hardly anyone else."

It was as Camilla had suspected from the moment that Edith Jessop had granted the request. She found herself unable to consider the dimensions of the difficulty because Edith Jessop hadn't stopped talking.

"All I hear when I'm with him is that you're a lady and I'm not. He used to eat my cooking with all the pleasure in the world, but now he says that no true lady will lower herself to cook."

Camilla was reminded of Vivien Malbot in Kent. Arthur's provisional wife-to-be had been taught by her late mother about the preparation of food, and her Aunt Malbot was proud of it. There was no point to mentioning that in front of the angry Edith Jessop. Indeed, if the red-haired girl wasn't halted in the midst of a verbal flight, her litany of complaints would proceed until the Drury Lane management once again revived *King Lear.*

"I can only tell you that nothing whatever has taken place between me and Mr. Royde that is of a romantic nature," Camilla assured the furious red-haired girl. "Nor will it ever take place, I'll be bound!"

Edith Jessop wasn't comforted. She hadn't sought out her nemesis with the intention of drawing comfort, and would have been dismayed to find herself feeling the slightest sympathy or liking for the aristocratic Camilla.

"But you must be leading Willie on," she charged.

"I have seen Mr. Royde only twice, one time at his establishment and another at Ascot."

"Oh yes, Ascot!" Another grievance had been touched on. Clearly Royde hadn't taken Edith to witness the occasion that represented the height of social elegance, hoping to make some contact with Camilla instead. That he had accomplished his goal to no profit would have been impossible for Camilla to say in a manner that might convince the other. "You flirted with a man who isn't of your class."

Once again there was no benefit in a denial. Camilla contented herself with tight-lipped silence and hoped that her own sharpness would make itself felt.

It probably did, causing yet another outburst. "You don't care if you hurt others," Edith Jessop insisted.

Camilla checked the first defensive words that crossed her mind. On Edith Jessop's level of society she, too, was involved in the search for a man whose interest in her was the unquestioned proof of Queen Vickie–like respectability. Instead of making do with one of the gents she could almost certainly have lured, Edith also wanted one man in particular. Camilla's older sister had settled for the first who asked, but Edith, like Camilla, instinctively knew the merits of choosing with care. Edith Jessop was more of a sister in spirit than Louise could ever have been.

"If you have come here to call me names, then your object is accomplished," Camilla said, speaking coolly when she wanted to shake the other girl in a fury and then embrace her in friendship. "If you have any other purpose, you had best tell me what it is."

Edith Jessop looked fully at Camilla's face and saw enough in the eyes to divert the channel of her speech into reasonable terms.

"You must tell Willie what you have said to me." Edith shook her head rather than adding the title "Miss," unwilling to give Camilla that courtesy. "Tell my Willie that you can never have any serious interest in him. Tell him as how you won't have a thing to do with him."

"I said as much to him once." Camilla had attempted to convey that thought at Ascot in mid-month. Royde's only response had been to insist that there must be further contact between them.

"He must have thought you were coquetting."

"I wasn't."

"Tell him in such a way that he'll believe it," Edith insisted.

The suggestion made sense for her and Edith as well. It was tempting to remark that Will Royde's amatory interest wouldn't necessarily alight upon Edith again as a consequence. His contacts with a different level of society could have caused Royde to set his goals on drawing closer to a female of that type, not realizing that never was he likely to be entirely at ease with a gentle young woman.

Nevertheless Edith's suggestion remained proper and suitable.

"I will make the attempt once more," she promised.

Edith nodded. She tried to speak, but could still not bring herself to offer thanks or the slightest expression of regard. A straightforward girl was Edith Jessop, like her or not, and meeting her had been refreshing. Camilla found herself hoping that some good qualities in William Royde made him worthy of Edith.

Camilla occupied her mind during the remainder of Mr. Balfe's musicalized fiction about love and happiness by thinking of how to accomplish the objective on which she had determined. Writing a note to Will Royde would be useless, as

it certainly wasn't going to carry the conviction of a personal
statement repeated forcefully. She did not know, nor was it
important, where he might be reached in the daytime. Therefore it became necessary that she seek him out at his gambling
premises and make her feelings unmistakably clear.

A cohort would be desirable company for this expedition.
Edith Jessop was ruled out for the most obvious reason. A
friend might be impelled to gossip. Arthur would gladly have
been of aid, but he was in such a wax since returning from
Kent that his services were unlikely to be of the least use. She
never considered asking her father's help.

Because of her disdain for so many ritualized forms of
behavior, she accepted the idea almost willingly that the matter would have to be handled by Miss Camilla Fairfield alone.

Nothing could be done till the family had once more returned to Lower Brook Street and Camilla officially sought
her bed. It took longer than expected for the reason that
Louise and her wastrel of a husband returned to Lower Brook
Street for a stirrup cup before proceeding to whatever private
quarrel was currently occupying them when they were alone.
Camilla put the best face on it.

Eventually Louise and her cargo took their leave. A grateful
Arthur yawned all the way upstairs to bed. Camilla said her
good-nights almost immediately afterwards and hurried up to
her room. Her royal blue had been cleaned and ironed by the
indefatigable Annie, but there remained the slightest intractable miff of Ginger, the horse, in that material. She didn't
mind. The color was unsuitable in the first place, and a slight
odor would detract even further when she confronted Royde.
For the balance of this particular night Camilla Fairfield didn't
want to be considered a comely young woman.

Her darkest mantle would offer sufficient outer covering.
With this in hand she opened her door and looked down the
hall. No one was in sight. Walking swiftly, she proceeded
down the back stairs and out to the thoroughfare and the first
empty cab in sight.

"Take me to Royde's on Bennet Street," she instructed.

"A gambling 'ell." The driver sniffed.

"Take me there without further discussion," Camilla said crisply, although enjoying his Victoria-like disapproval because the implications behind it were totally unfounded.

"Very well, miss." The driver sniffed once more, then issued instructions to his pair of horses and the cab was under way.

CHAPTER FOURTEEN

Camilla settled with the driver as they reached the house next to Royde's, drawing coins from her ample reticule and shutting it before she stepped out. The building that housed William Royde's establishment looked no less respectable than the houses closely set beside it.

The orderly walked in front of Royde's premises, keeping an eye out for any cluster of Bobby Peel's police force. He remembered Camilla, smiled, doffed his cap respectfully, and opened the door for her.

In the small anteroom she retained her cloak, then paused. "I would like a mask."

"Certainly, miss." The attendant cocked his head, considering Camilla's bright blond hair and blue eyes. "What color, miss? White? An azure, perhaps?"

"Neither. I will wear the darkest purple mask in your hoard."

The attendant protested, "But your coloring demands a lighter shade in accessories."

"I insist on purple." There was a certain perverse pleasure in dressing badly. One look at the mask in place confirmed the correctness of her choice for the desired goal. It made her eyes look the color of chimney soot and seemed to cause her chin to jut out even further than nature, in a burst of unkindness, had intended. She felt certain that Will Royde's previously justified opinion of her charms was shortly going to plummet.

The two gambling rooms hadn't changed from Camilla's

visit earlier in the month. Players in a state of feverish absorption stared down at different tables. Employees of the establishment urged them to risk still more money on a turn of the cards, a throw of dice. The only difference of which she was aware, and that with a distinct feeling of irritation, consisted in the absence of William Royde.

She stopped one of the waiters, who carried a refreshment tray parallel with the top of his bald head, preventing the poor man from moving.

"Where is Mr. Royde?"

The waiter, a middle-aged man whose palm strained under the weight of the tray, courteously looked around. Camilla stepped to one side in the meantime, giving him the space he needed.

The man said after a moment, "Mr. R., 'e mout be in 'is hoffice."

And he left in a justifiable hurry.

Another factotum directed Camilla out of the farthest of the gambling areas and up the stairs. At a landing in the hall she passed a door open on an empty room. In that space, she supposed, the staff would hide boards, dice, and cards in case of a sudden raid by Bobby Peel's minions. If the police couldn't prove that illegal gaming had been in progress, they might consequently be sued for wrongful entry and trespass and whatever further infractions a hungry solicitor could add to a bill of particulars. As a result, it was rare indeed for the police to arrive unexpectedly at gambling hells like this one.

A closed door painted in forest green was located some ten feet past the ultimate step on the topmost level. Approaching footsteps could be heard on the other side. Before Camilla could knock, the door was opened swiftly.

"Ah!" There was a smile on Royde's thick lips, and his dark eyes lightened. "So you *have* come back! I'd had you looked out for, and the orderly just sent a boy to tell me that you are here."

He seemed not to care that she was dressed in colors that were strikingly inappropriate. If he thought of it at all, he considered that there was some outrageous new style in good society of which he wasn't yet aware.

Camilla drew back. Her reasons for bearding this lion, so well conceived at the outset, suddenly seemed trivial. Because of what he was allegedly saying to others about his feeling for her, it had now become clear that she never ought to have permitted herself to enter his premises again, by herself or even in company.

She would be wisest to make her point plain beyond doubt.

"I have to tell you irrevocably that I'll not have anything to do with you ever again, in this place or out of it."

His normally rigid posture had become slightly relaxed, both hands outstretched as if he was offering the run of the premises. Not one of Camilla's words had apparently made the least impression.

"You're here," he beamed. "That is of the greatest importance. It proves that you wanted to be with me again."

"Only to inform you that I have no intention of trafficking with you under any circumstances."

"But you came here yourself rather than sending a message or asking another to repeat your thoughts to me."

She was unable to say that it was a perception of urgency that had driven her to these straits. Clarifying the point would have involved discussing Edith Jessop, which she was entirely unwilling to do.

"Most important of all, you have again put on the mask and it is as Lady Fortune that you have come back," he added happily. "It proves that you have a certain feeling for me."

Not till she heard those unprovoked words was Camilla fully aware that the man was besotted with her and with her station in good society as well. For Camilla to make much of him in turn would be evidence of his worldly success. She felt sorry for Royde because he couldn't bring himself to accept what was actually so clear. At the same time she was making every effort to stifle her rage at him.

"I know now that you and I will become true friends," he insisted. "I do not wish to be forward at this time, to anticipate, but I feel that over the years I will be able to make you very happy."

Such complete misunderstanding would have appalled anyone else. Proof was certainly being offered that Edith Jessop had not tampered with the truth by insisting that Royde was deeply infatuated with Camilla. As consolation at this time, the knowledge of Edith's veracity was negligible.

"There must be some known human language that we both speak and in which it is possible for me to make myself clear."

"On the contrary. Everything has now been made entirely clear."

"Presumably if a policeman comes to arrest you, it would be obvious that he actually is asking you to replace Prince Albert as the consort of our Queen."

He laughed uncertainly, as if the humor of society women was beyond him. She had forgotten that humor of any sort was strange to Royde.

"The point I wish to make clear beyond peradventure of doubt is that I would have to be drugged with laudanum or worse before consenting to order my existence along the lines that you describe."

"When you are no longer drugged, you would be happy afterwards. How much it is going to please me that I can make every effort and be sure of that!"

He seemed totally deaf to her words and even to the crispness of her tones. It was possible to sympathize with his desire to change much of the life he led, but Camilla didn't want him doing so at her side. She was apparently not nearly as much the rebel as she sometimes considered herself.

"I cannot expect to gain approval for such a course from the peer who intends to marry me." Her last throw, so to speak, of the dice.

"He will curse himself for having lost to someone of greater basic worth."

"But I am now spoken for." It was a lie, though suitable for the occasion. "I am to be wed."

"To a man of 'noble' birth." Royde sneered like some actor on the Drury Lane stage. "His parents have forced him into offering for you, and your parents, in turn, are demanding that you accede to the wish."

It was almost comic to think how far from the truth his speculation had landed.

"I love him," she responded vehemently, and wondered if she was speaking about Trevor Drawhill.

"You're too fine to admit what is actually so, that you are being forced." His stubbornness was that of a fanatic. There was admiration for her in his voice.

She had endured sufficiently. Turning away from him was a gesture she performed with relief. Swiftly she proceeded to the staircase.

He spoke after her. "I remember now that I have read about your trouble in *Day's Doings*, the gossip journal. Of course I paid no attention. But I believe it is Trevor, the Duke of Strafford, who actually fancies you."

Her hand was on the rail of the staircase, and she was lowering her right foot to the next step.

"Well, I can make sure that the Duke of Strafford is nobbled in this competition," Royde said fiercely. "Some of my larky friends will see to him if it's necessary. Yes, they will certainly see to him."

Never before had Camilla heard anyone speak along those lines, but she was aware that violence against Trevor was being threatened. Camilla raised herself and turned back, not knowing whether she was going to make a plea for Royde to abstain from the course he had outlined or make threats in return.

Nor was there an opportunity for her to speak. Royde had hurried up behind her and now suddenly folded Camilla in his arms. She felt his lips on hers. She struggled against him with all the strength she could muster.

As it happened, he released her rather quickly. Long afterwards she was inclined to wonder if it wasn't the slight smell of horse upon her dress that startled him into accelerating his timetable.

Freed now, she slapped him on a cheek. He made a sound that might have been a laugh or a bark for all she knew, then raised a hand. But all he did then was to smooth the offended area. Most likely that was an afterthought, his first impulse having been to strike back at his fair tormentor. Somewhere he had heard or been told that gentlemen never behaved so logically, a memory which had caused him to refrain from the vengeance he almost certainly craved.

Not a moment too soon Camilla turned and ran down the stairs, condemning herself because her generosity towards Edith Jessop had helped expose Trevor to possible severe difficulty, that he might shortly be set upon by footpads in the hire of a man whom no one could ever have called Willie in a truly affectionate manner. Trevor could suffer serious injuries as a result. She wanted nothing more than to reach Trevor immediately and warn him against Royde. She could not be sure if Trevor found himself in London and was without the least notion where he might be located. At this time she had no idea about what to do.

It was most unfortunate for her peace of mind, as a result, that she didn't choose to reenter the gambling rooms and linger until Trevor Drawhill arrived.

CHAPTER FIFTEEN

The course of six lives was to be altered on that night for several reasons, among the most important being that Arthur Fairfield was weary.

For this much Arthur could offer excellent reasons. He had waked up early in the morning, an activity unheard of in his previous existence. After a quickly devoured breakfast he had raced down to the financial section of the City. Here, instead of making quips at the expense of those friends who were employed in helping to set the course of empire, he had humbly asked that he be allowed to become one of them. In all cases he had been swiftly rejected either by the so-called friends or by elders who knew of the course his life had taken until that point and didn't believe his intentions were in the least serious. Not knowing Arthur too well, each of them scoffed at the power of true love to reform a man beyond recognition.

As if to prove that he could engage in the activities of outwardly respectable people, Arthur had tortured himself further by attending an *opérette* in his family's presence. During the course of that entertainment it was possible to see on the stage that a stranger with important friends could make matters right for deserving young lovers. Had he been in a more questioning frame of mind, Arthur would have immediately discerned the differences between a fairy tale and the ugly reality which he had been freshly experiencing.

On the way home it occurred to him that it might be possible to inquire of Trevor, the Duke of Strafford, whether any further assistance was possible in this campaign. He had rejected that course in talking to Camilla at Kent, but he was no longer inclined to dismiss any possible source of the aid that he required. More importantly, Trevor had been acquainted with Vivien since childhood, so he certainly wished her well and was likely to extend himself to be of help.

It was worth some discussion with his father, but Louise and her husband were in their company and such a consultation apparently had to be put off. Worse yet, the Passys invaded their home afterwards. Arthur anticipated some trouble in speaking with the guv'nor, but the females congregated in one corner of the large sitting room to discuss fashions and Anthony was shortly comatose. The conversation was soon being held in low tones.

"You wish to consult Strafford, do you?" Father considered. "Certainly the thought is worth the most serious reflection."

It was the sort of neutral encouragement of which the guv'nor seemed to make a specialty. Arthur resumed his cogitating while Sir Osric continued to encourage his son without actually saying a word for or against the intended course of action.

Arthur waited courteously until Louise and her useless husband departed. In spite of himself he yawned prodigiously on his way upstairs and to his bedroom. In the hallway it occurred to him that he would be wisest not to brook further delays. Weary though he felt, he ought to put this matter in train immediately. By way of an incentive, he realized that he had no idea how much longer Trevor would be staying in London.

Unlike his younger sister, he knew that Trevor kept a suite of rooms at the Albany, on the north side of Piccadilly. To reach this haven a cab would be necessary. Arthur left his parents' home quietly and without a cloak. He didn't know that if he had delayed his departure for a while he might have encountered Camilla, who was also searching the street for a cab.

His mission at the Albany was brief and fruitless. Trevor wasn't available. A mutual friend let him know that Trevor

had gone agaming, but wasn't sure which of a dozen establish-
ments was being favored by his custom.

Arthur walked outside slowly, recollecting that Trevor had
spoken with particular approval about an establishment in
Bennet Street. Royde's, as he recollected. William Royde's
gambling hell.

The place wasn't so far from here, being on the first street
at the right as one turned down St. James's from Piccadilly.
Arthur was in no condition to trust himself to walk and keep
up that brisk stride which was necessary in avoiding villains
and passing demireps who shrilly offered unwanted favors.
Another cab was necessary.

During this jaunt he fell asleep and was awakened by the
driver bellowing down at him from the customary perch. Arthur staggered out, paid his fee, and eased past the scowling
orderly and the purse-lipped cloakroom attendant.

Upon entering the gambling rooms he allowed himself a
slow look around. His hopes sank. Trevor Drawhill, the Duke
of Strafford, the object of Arthur's knightly quest, was not
among those in attendance on the goddess of chance.

A friend was lurking at the chemmy table, and Arthur approached warily.

"Are you expecting Trevor Drawhill?" he whispered.

"Not particularly," said Arthur's friend. "Are you?"

Arthur made an impatient gesture. "I thought you might
have some reason to know if Trevor will come by. Both of you
sit in the Lords and he might've spoken to you about it."

"Lord Pam speaks to me on occasion, but I couldn't tell
anybody if John Bull is going to have a war within the next two
weeks."

"Friends, as I always say, are invaluable," Arthur sighed.

He was straightening up when he heard some sobbing female rushing down the hall stairs and away from Willie
Royde's office. It was easy enough to guess what had happened on the upper level, Arthur felt sure. Royde was a heart-
breaker among the females of a certain low class, and probably he had thrown some young lady over. He would have said
crisply that never again did he want to see her. It was a com-

monplace happening in Willie Royde's circles, Arthur supposed, and much worthier of being the subject of an *opérette*
than whatever it was that he had witnessed earlier tonight at
the Drury Lane.

He considered the possibility of leaving to investigate the
clientele at Ned Boucher's place on New Burlington Street. It
was the Duke's second favorite hell. Other friends, however,
entering and seeing him, took it for granted that Arthur had
come here to revel and insisted on his joining them. In vain
did he clarify his reason for entering these premises. No one
had seen Trevor during the night; none knew where he might
be found. Indeed, a handsome young woman in the group
owned up to never having met Trevor at all.

Upon being offered a chance to slake his undoubted thirst,
Arthur accepted the opportunity to show goodwill, in turn, to
these friends. The cup of warm negus didn't perk him up. The
effect, as he ought to have anticipated, was precisely the opposite. Feeling warm and relaxed, he rested by taking a seat at
his friends' hazard table, but fell asleep promptly. Only when
he started to snore was he wakened, and then by an elbow
slicing into one of his more vulnerable ribs. He called out,
which was an irritating sound to the gamblers.

Keenly aware that he had committed a *faux pas* of august
proportions, Arthur clambered to his feet. He was ready to
leave. A quick look around to locate one favored friend to
whom he wanted to bid farewell was enough to pull him up
short. Trevor Drawhill was sitting at a far table, immersed in a
game of écarté.

Arthur knew well that no man could be approached for a
long discussion while in the throes of surrendering money.
He stared. Catching Trevor's eyes, he offered an encouraging
smile. Trevor startled him with a gesture requesting him to
wait.

Having succeeded beyond expectations, Arthur wondered
why the gods had suddenly smiled upon him. Soon enough he
realized that he found himself in a new difficulty. Trevor was
fond of Camilla, and there had been some quarrel between
them, as Arthur vaguely remembered hearing. Trevor proba-

bly felt that Miss Fairfield's brother could be a stern influence persuading Cammie to a reconciliation. Not having been blessed with sisters of his own, the Duke had no idea how unmanageable a young female relative could become when she took the bit between her teeth.

The écarté game eventually concluded. Trevor handed over his doubloons, then spoke a few brief words to the more successful players and a rather distant Willie Royde. After which he joined Arthur, who was leaning against the far door.

" 'Pon my word, I would have lost another fifty of the blunt if you hadn't rescued me," Trevor said by way of greeting. He led the way outside past the orderly. Under the bright moon that flooded Bennet Street Trevor paused once more. "And how is your charming sister, may I ask?"

"Camilla is very well." Arthur decided to pour the flattery on. "She speaks of no one but you. She sighs and repines and is inconsolable."

Actually he had been too deeply involved with his own difficulties to be aware of what Camilla might be feeling. His younger sister could have been pining after the Great Cham of Tartary for all of him.

Trevor's sudden skepticism reflected Arthur's uncertainty. "I understand that she was at the theater much earlier tonight with all the family."

"Oh yes, yes, that's true." At the moment Arthur had to strain himself to recollect the episode. "But underneath it all, her heart was breaking."

Arthur was aware of Trevor Drawhill sharply examining him.

"There is some favor you wish from me or you wouldn't seek me out at this time," Trevor concluded. "Cut the gammon and get to the spinach. How can I be of service?"

Arthur didn't have energy enough to expand upon protestations that his feelings for Trevor at this moment were those of true comradeship and the meeting had been entirely accidental. Without further delay he discussed Vivien's implicit conviction that he must be a useful member of the City, and that the circumstance needed to be proved before her family would consent to have the banns put up in anticipation of the wedding. To save time, as Arthur told himself, he didn't add that he had claimed he was already employed in that fashion.

"And you expect that I can help you." Trevor shrugged. "I have very few longtime acquaintances in London, as I should think you know."

Arthur nodded. While talking to Camilla over the recent weekend he had made that point himself. He didn't need to say that it was still possible to hope against hope.

"All I can see for it is for me to discuss it with anyone whose ear I can obtain," Trevor added. "You, who are far better acquainted in these precincts, have been doing similarly with no results."

"None today," Arthur admitted.

"Well, your efforts have only got under way," Trevor pointed out. "Perhaps matters will improve with time. Was there anyone at Royde's who might be of some use?"

"No one whatever."

"Present company included, I fear. But I will make the effort." Trevor's voice grew softer. "You seem tired."

Arthur was bone-weary. In the past he had spent clusters of twenty-four-hour periods without sleep while in the pursuit of pleasure and remained fresh for some hours afterwards. A similar amount of consecutive time occupied in a search for respectability, however, would have been enough to sap the energy of a Russian wolf.

"We must find a cab for you," Trevor insisted.

At the moment Arthur welcomed such assistance. He leaned against a gas lamppost while Trevor paced out beyond the sidewalk. Watching through bleary eyes, Arthur saw that the other man missed two cabs. The Duke in motion wasn't the most alert of creatures, it seemed.

Neither man observed the three miscreants who silently walked out of the basement floor of William Royde's building and looked around. One of them nodded decisively. The Duke, who had recently strode out of the gambling rooms, was busily looking for a cab. Some drunkard lounged against the nearby lamppost.

"Hoy! You!" The first man spoke.

Trevor, having paused in his peregrinations, turned. The beefiest of these men had a prominent gold tooth and wore a beaver hat with tight-fitting clothes that looked almost like a rig-out that the Prince Consort might have designed for use by men in the Navy. A second man, missing most of his teeth and dressed similarly, stood at the first one's side. The third, not in range of light, kept a short distance behind them.

"You're the Jewk?"

Trevor understood that he was being asked about his identity. Appraisingly his eyes narrowed and he stood with arms akimbo, waiting to hear what the beefiest man, the one whose teeth would make his words clearer, might want.

Arthur did not share any doubt. A Londoner to the fingertips, one look at the spokesman and his phalanx of cohorts was enough to convince him that Trevor had in some way run afoul of three ruffians. This difficulty offered a chance to protect Trevor, earning gratitude that might be useful in his own quest. No other stimulus would have galvanized Arthur into even an approximation of energy.

"And what would it mean to you?" he asked.

The toothless one sputtered, "Stow it, Cyril!"

The name was intended as an insult, of course. Arthur retorted by making a pair of fists.

"You three get busy elsewhere," he said, glancing over a shoulder to see if Trevor was impressed by his forcefulness. "Do that, or I'll know how to arrange all of you."

Trevor, perhaps thinking that he had been silently consulted, put in with smoothness, "I doubt if any of these three men are intending fisticuffs."

Arthur was inclined to agree, primarily because at least two of them were wearing clothes so tight as to deny comfortable movement to someone involved in a street brawl. Therefore a show of greater anger could do no harm to anyone.

"You'll all get knuckled if you don't leave quickly," he promised.

The one with the gold tooth looked contemptuous but said nothing, and turned to Trevor.

"You listen 'ere, Jewk," he began.

Arthur put in angrily, "Do you dare to address a peer of the Queen's realm in those terms?"

He had gone too far by once more preventing the other from relaying whatever message he had been paid to deliver. The spokesman glanced at his closest companion, who instantly detached himself.

Arthur had time to slip into the boxing stance he had learned from no less a champion than "Gentleman" Jackson. In sparring with the Gentleman some years after the latter's retirement from the squared circle, Arthur had been effective. It never occurred to him that Jackson might have been holding back his best efforts even at that time.

The thought did filter into his mind now, but only after the toothless one, tight clothes and all, punched Arthur in the jaw and dropped him to the pavement.

Arthur struggled to his feet. He heard the sound of a fist crashing against bone. It was clear to him after a moment that the ruffians were taking flight.

From the quick glance at the payment he realized that Trevor was not recumbent. A pair of expensive boots did come into view at second glance, their owner obviously standing. Trevor stopped puffing air against a briefly inflamed knuckle and hurried to Arthur.

The latter asked admiringly, "Where did you learn to use your fives like that?"

"Oh, one acquires such skills in the country," Trevor said, making light of his accomplishment on account of Arthur's recent showing. Nor did he add that the men hadn't intended violence, and only his successful resort to fighting had driven them off with their message undelivered. "Are you able to walk?"

"Certainly." Arthur took two steps and briefly lost his balance.

"I am of the opinion that you will require an escort to Lower Brook Street. Consider that my services are offered."

"The family will be worried if we are seen arriving together."

"Not necessarily," Trevor remarked. "They will simply be convinced that you resumed your nocturnal impersonation of the Caliph of Bagdad, and that you drank one or two over the allotted eight as a consquence, and then suffered a slight accident. Is that not so?"

"I think I see a cab," said Arthur.

CHAPTER SIXTEEN

Camilla did not encounter her brother again until the wait for supper the next evening. Arthur had slept late and spent only a few hours in the City, a circumstance which he justified to his younger sister by telling her what had taken place on the previous night and why.

Watching him pace the small sitting room on the second floor, Camilla felt regret that Trevor had been near the house early this morning and she hadn't known of it. She had left a message for him with an attendant at the House of Lords, warning about William Royde's lack of goodwill towards him, and now realized that Trevor had been aware of the position since last night.

"On the whole," she said, "I consider that what you have told me is very encouraging."

Arthur was looking at her as if she had lost her senses. Dinner was announced immediately, allowing him no time to offer his opinion.

An event of some interest had been planned for that night. A portrait painted by Louise's father-in-law was to be hung, with works by artists now deceased, in the National Gallery at Trafalgar Square. Relations by marriage, such as the Fairfields, were properly expected to put in an appearance.

None of the Fairfields looked forward to a few hours of hearing the painter bellow and snort. Camilla expected Sir Victor to be particularly galled because an example of his work had been sold by the surviving relative of former owners, so that his own profit from this purchase by the Gallery was nonexistent. In this prediction Camilla turned out to be correct.

Eight-thirty found Camilla in her most discreet rose merino, walking on low-heeled shoes on the Grecian portico that had been taken intact from Carlton House only five years ago, back in '38.

"I wish you hadn't chosen to wear *that*," Mamma said quietly at Camilla's side. "A plethora of young men should be present for your inspection, as you ought to have anticipated. Probably most of these will have some appreciation for the finer things of life, which brings them here."

"Young men such as Arthur, you mean?" Camilla smiled. Her brother, acting once again because of a family obligation, was walking ahead. His eyes were downcast, though, as if they might encounter a work of art if he wasn't careful.

"We shall hope for the best," Lady Fairfield said majestically.

Beyond the hall was a carpeted staircase that led to different vestibules. Men and women strolled this area, talking. References were made to Dutch and Tuscan schools, among others. The men were older, and those with some youth remaining in their bodies were accompanied by wives. Mamma's expectations had erred, as often happened, on the side of optimism.

In the area devoted to the works of British painters, the Fairfields found Sir Victor speaking critically of a Gainsborough nature scene at his left and venting even greater spleen on the painting that showed the Thames near Twickenham. Sir Victor's own attempts to paint scenes of nature had been notoriously unsuccessful, and the sight of these highly praised works offered ample nourishment to his natural foul temper.

Turning to a work by Hogarth, Sir Victor opined loudly that he disagreed with that scribbler who had referred to him as an affirmative Hogarth of the upper classes. Nevertheless the painter spoke those words with the greatest possible clarity. A deaf old lady studying an Orcagna in the farthest vestibule could probably have made out every word of the praise that Sir Victor had received.

"I felt sure that you would attend on this occasion," said Trevor, approaching Camilla from the side of a Zoffany painting. "I owe you my best thanks because of your having left a message for me at the Lords."

"Not at all." Camilla was unable to control the pounding of her heart and felt certain that he must be aware of it. "I understand that my strictures were needless."

"The perils that you envisaged for me were considerably overdrawn, as it happens, but the communication did help to prove your concern for me."

"I am often moved by the plight of my fellow creatures," Camilla said softly.

"Yours is a forgiving spirit," Trevor told her gallantly, almost as if there had been no brief pause in the colloquy. It was impossible to know whether he had flushed, his handsome face always being lightly tanned.

She sensed Mamma stiffening, no doubt in disapproval of Trevor. As if from a distance Camilla heard Mamma talking briefly to Arthur, who had almost certainly been gestured over to join them. Mamma proceeded to walk off more noisily than usual. So great was Lady Fairfield's current dislike of Trevor that she almost certainly couldn't bring herself to speak or be in proximity to him.

Arthur suddenly cleared his throat. "Cammie, it is time for you to greet Louise and Anthony, who are in conversation with Father and Mother. Your pardon, Trevor."

"And *your* pardon," said a new voice. "All of you."

In the first startled moment of identifying William Royde, Camilla didn't doubt that he had also guessed that the Fairfields, and perhaps Trevor, would be among those present at this celebration.

He wore an impeccable dark cutaway and loose tie over a white shirt, but his striped "lightning" trousers were far in advance of acceptable style. His dark eyes burned on Camilla as if no one else was actually in the room, causing her to stiffen even more than otherwise at memory of her previous encounter with this fiend from hell. She was unwilling to leave Trevor's presence, but made a point of turning from Royde. It did seem as if she and almost everyone else she knew wanted nothing to do with at least one other person of her acquaintance.

Royde, sounding impervious, addressed himself to Trevor. "I believe there was a misunderstanding last night, Your Grace, and it involved you."

Arthur permitted some sound to escape his lips.

"And you, too, Arthur, of course." It was noteworthy that Royde was far more at ease with a virtual crony. Arthur must have been a better client of such gambling hells as Royde's than even the startled Camilla had realized. Perhaps he had therefore become so tired of routine dissipation that his happiness with Vivien Malbot, if it could be arranged, was likely to be permanent.

"You put the matter in a temperate way," Trevor said at last. "Sir Osric Fairfield himself could hardly improve on your choice of locutions."

Royde continued, "Some gentlemen in my employ came to see you, Your Grace. They were not clothed for battle as none was intended."

"But it was offered and accepted, however. Despite excruciating difficulty because of their habiliments, a *brouhaha* was arranged, so to speak."

Arthur said reproachfully, "You shouldn't have sent them out."

Royde, stung, offered an accusation of his own. "And you shouldn't have taken such a high-and-mighty air with Ernie. You know the way Ernie is, Arthur. He can be sensitive."

Arthur, who hadn't recognized his assailant and wouldn't have been able to put a name to him at the best of times, refrained from shouting. The restraint was intended as a courtesy to other guests of the National Gallery. Royde, probably misinterpreting it as intended for his sake alone, nodded gratefully.

"My point is, Your Grace," he said, having turned his attentions back to Trevor, "that my workers were incited to a course they wouldn't otherwise have taken. I certainly don't want you or anyone else to think that such events are customary in or near my place of business."

Trevor still felt so put upon that even the apology left him cool. "Then I take it that nothing similar is going to happen again to Mr. Fairfield if he is ever injudicious enough to set foot near Bennet Street again."

Royde's newly hostile tone was an acknowledgment that he had failed to mollify the peer. "Nothing along that line will occur to you or a friend, Your Grace, as long as there is no further clash of goals between the two of us."

Only Camilla, who had come to know Trevor during this month, understood that the peer was genuinely puzzled.

"You may be aware, Your Grace, that I sent my men to make it clear that your interest in Miss Fairfield is not welcome."

Trevor said drily, "Miss Fairfield may not concur in that opinion."

"She will."

"You are no doubt aware that she and I have been in each other's company quite often in recent weeks."

He was keeping up the game that he and Camilla had been playing under society's approving glance. This time the stakes were higher. Camilla's future with some man of her own choice was certainly involved, as was the Duke's own prestige. Under no circumstances would Trevor Drawhill retreat in the face of some villain's aggression.

Carefully he added, "We, Miss Fairfield and I, may be on the point of making a decision along those lines."

"I am advising Your Grace what form the decision must take, for your own welfare."

"Such concern is deeply appreciated."

Royde apparently gave no indication of being cast down by that sardonic comment.

At which point Trevor made a cutting remark that was to have serious consequences. "It is unfortunate to see a gambler who doesn't know that he has lost."

Royde was stung, his face coloring. "I will prove that there has been no loss on my part."

"Indeed."

"Yes indeed. We will settle this quarrel and prove who is the wiser man, and therefore best suited to Miss Fairfield."

"With what means do you propose to accomplish that?"

"By gaming," Royde snapped. "And the stakes will consist of your withdrawal from the courtship of Miss Fairfield as soon as the results are clear."

Camilla wanted to protest that she would not allow a contest on such terms, but His Grace was already responding.

"And if *you* lose, I expect the same treatment."

"I will communicate with you about the time and place to settle our differences."

Without another word he was gone, leaving Camilla and Arthur to stare wonderingly at each other while Trevor took her hand in a strong grip. He turned away to speak with Mr. Benjamin D'Israeli, an M.P., and his wife, who had recently entered the exhibition area side by side.

A silent and even stunned Arthur took her away for a brief but necessary conversation with Louise and a sullen Anthony. Sir Victor, intruding on anyone who dared to hold a conversation of which he wasn't the center of attention, made his usual booming noises. Camilla escaped gratefully when Sir Osric chose to distract the noisy artist.

Mamma stood in her path. A look of dawning comprehension was enlivening Lady Fairfield's features.

"You are fond of Trevor Drawhill, are you not? Genuinely fond of him?"

Camilla nodded.

Mamma offered no word of protest in spite of antagonism towards Trevor for leading her daughter in a wicked deception of all their loving relatives.

"Do you think he will offer for you?"

"I don't know what will happen."

This was no time to speak about the occurrences of the last few minutes, let alone the reasons for them. Questions from Mamma would have kept Camilla rooted in place for the remainder of the night. Nonetheless she was determined to speak later with this softer and more understanding version of Mamma, to tell everything before the odious event took place.

"You are apparently off to rejoin him now," Mamma said with a soft smile that Camilla didn't know was reflecting memories of her own maidenhood. "With so many others in the room, I cannot believe that a chaperone will be necessary to overhear your words."

She found Trevor standing south by west of a Romney that showed some sickly boy sitting on the lap of his smug mother. A while ago he had greeted Mr. Gladstone and Lord Stanley, and was clearly waiting with impatience for her to come back to him.

"I will not be gamed for," Camilla said spiritedly as soon as she was in earshot. "I am not a coin to be won or a cake to be given as a prize at some county fair."

"Indisputably, you are neither of those," Trevor conceded, pausing only for a graceful nod in the direction of the devil-may-care Baron Lyndhurst. "But when I consider what choices are open to you I see rather a small field."

She threw her head back defiantly. "One alternative is open to me if such a contest does indeed take place and he wins it. That is to ignore him entirely. It is what I would plan upon doing if that eventuality is realized."

"In which case he might not hesitate to keep you from any possible alliance with another," Trevor pointed out. "By violence, if need be."

"But he cannot possibly do such a hellish thing!"

"Who is there to keep him from venting his spite? He will always be somewhere else when an actual incident occurs. There is a trade term for that condition in his circles, but I forget what it is."

"I cannot believe this! It is monstrous, like a curse out of the Middle Ages, like the *droit du seigneur* or something equally vile." An even more awful thought intruded upon her alarm. "And if he loses, will such a man be able to abide by any rules whatever?"

In this matter, as it happened, Trevor was encouraging. "I believe so, yes. He does accept the principles of gaming, and if it became a matter of public notice that he had not bowed to the result of a contest along those lines, I feel quite certain that his career would be adversely affected. And unless I am enormously mistaken, our friend knows it as well as I do."

"If he loses, you will be the victor," she said, having chosen the words with more care than they appeared to deserve.

He understood that a question was being asked indirectly. "In the event of my triumph, I will make every effort to take the prize I have won, which is the right to court you."

"You mean so that you can impress the *haut ton* with being occupied, and that you shouldn't be bothered by a display of female candidates for your hand."

She was aware of his sudden probing look at her, as if comprehending, after the long delay, that she had been hurt to a greater extent than she would ever bring herself to admit.

"No," he said softly. "I will be occupied, to use that word, exactly as a clergyman would prefer."

She couldn't help looking incredulous.

He spoke again before she could press for clarification. "I have greatly missed the pleasures of your company and want to experience them daily and with the greatest possible keenness."

She met his nile green eyes. "In that case, you must win the forthcoming contest."

"I shall do so."

The pleasure of mutual understanding caused Trevor to make immediate closer contact. He took a step nearer to her and his arms suddenly circled her waist.

Camilla looked up and returned his smile. His lips pressed down urgently on hers. She didn't know or care how long the contact lasted. Only when he reluctantly let her go was she aware of a deep hush from the nearest witnesses.

"That should prove to you how sincere I am," he said.

Camilla didn't question it.

CHAPTER SEVENTEEN

To describe the chaotic minutes that followed with even the least accuracy would require a pen touched by genius. The chronicler, having paused in apparently endless agony with quill in hand, can offer only the lightest sketch of the activities of major participants at that time.

Trevor, aware of the startled and disapproving looks on all sides, promised to be in touch with Camilla very shortly and took his *congé*.

William Royde stood in silent anger at what he felt was his opponent's squalid attempt to have his way with the well-brought-up young woman Royde was determined to wed.

Camilla was shortly confronted by Mamma, who insisted on taking her home. They were joined momentarily by Sir Osric and Arthur. No one spoke during the carriage ride to Lower Brook Street, but Camilla did let out a furtive chuckle at the thought of Sir Victor being outraged because the attention of many people had shifted from him for even a few moments.

In the upstairs sitting room in the family home, Lady Fairfield, too bemused for clambering out of evening satin, questioned her daughter. She desired information rather than the opportunity to convey disapproval. Camilla responded by a keen analysis of the events of those last moments at the National Gallery. Lady Fairfield looked awed.

"Are you saying—are you telling me—that two men will be gaming for you?"

As Camilla had succinctly conveyed just this intelligence, she could only nod at the direct question.

"How envious *le monde* will be!" Lady Fairfield enthused, clasping her hands joyfully. "I cannot conceive but that Amelia Tweeding will turn green while Janet Dowd will favor a light puce. There will be colorful times in the sitting rooms of London's eligible young and their maternal parents."

Camilla's own features resembled persimmon in shading when she heard her mother treat of the forthcoming encounter as a joyful occasion.

"Trevor will be gaming with a man who earns his living by being conversant with gamesters of all sorts and must therefore know more of the subject than he does. The possibility is a lively one that he may not emerge as the winner."

"Yes, there is that consideration," Lady Fairfield admitted more soberly, returning herself to Camilla's good graces. "Can this fellow, Royde, prevent you from being married to the man of your choice?"

"Trevor seems to feel strongly that he could."

"And as your brother experienced some violence at the hands of Royde's lackeys, he would almost certainly agree." Lady Fairfield paused. "I could not have recognized the man, but had I done so I would have given London cause for gossip of a different nature."

Of that much Camilla felt no doubt.

There wasn't any further information to be gleaned by Mamma in these *pourparlers.* Consequently she returned downstairs, where she consulted with her husband over this difficulty. Sir Osric was moved, but saw no way in which he could offer his dear daughter the slightest aid. Lady Fairfield was dismayed by his ineffectiveness, but far from surprised.

Morning brought a contenting sun and pleasant breezes. Noontime brought, more importantly, a note from Trevor.

After expressing his regard for her family and asking that he be remembered to its components, he proceeded to discuss the most important difficulties facing him and Camilla.

I am to meet William Royde in his establishment at ten o'clock this night, whereupon we will game along the lines that were indicated in yesterday's discussion at the Gallery. At this time I have no further information.

Be assured of my strong feelings for you.

Camilla ran her fingers over those last words again and again.

Arthur had listened open-mouthed to Mother's account of his sister's travail. He felt deep sympathy for Camilla, then allowed himself to discern one consolation that applied to his own difficulty. At the very least he wasn't being called upon to game for Vivien's hand. All the same, he hadn't won Vivien yet.

In addressing himself to the latter condition, he had once more set out to find a position for himself in the bustling world of finance.

No other attitude would have normally caused him to venture into Cockspur Street, with its odious smells traveling from the Thames, its warrens of shipping offices, and the clutter of stone hitching posts that made it almost impossible to take ten steps without finding some barrier against the midriff.

The Gardyne Bank, which he had heard about from Mrs. Winifred Malbot over a dinner out at Kent, was located just above Whitehall. It seemed like a distinct possibility that Arthur could make representations to the gentleman in charge and later inform Vivien's aunt that he had entered a new sphere of employment at a fresh location.

Mr. Gardyne was accessible, a tall and hawk-nosed man in silver-rimmed glasses. He expressed pleasure in meeting Mr. Fairfield, of whose father he had read in certain august publications. The mention of Mrs. Malbot's name brought some wariness, but the smiles and nods continued. Mr. Gardyne apparently felt that Arthur's visit was one of the high points of his existence. Unfortunately he could offer no possibility of employment on a high level in the precincts of Gardyne's Bank.

"However, I think that you might fare better at Mr. Derek Wolverstone's establishment. He is younger than I, and experimental in outlook. Of course you know of Wolverstone's Bank on Bruton Street."

"Of course."

Arthur thanked the man with sincerity, as he had been courteously received. He could hardly wait to leave, however, the business office being so constricted by desks and chairs. There was hardly place for a gentleman to move in, it seemed. Adapting to the atmosphere of commerce was going to offer some difficulties, but about these he was currently unwilling to speculate.

Mr. Gardyne amiably accompanied Arthur over to the reception area. A sudden gasp from a woman caused Arthur to look to the right. His jaw dropped. Vivien, who had called out, was sitting with her aunt on two of the chairs.

He took several steps towards her. Accordingly Vivien rose and hurried in his direction. It was fortunate for Arthur's mental equilibrium that they stopped short of touching one another.

"I didn't think that the pursuit of your duties would bring you here," Vivien said, her merry eyes round with astonishment. In russet with bright trimmings, she looked fresh and typically lovely.

"A man goes where he must." Arthur detested lying, and to Vivien in particular. He spoke quickly. "I happen to be very busy at this time."

"Certainly I don't want to interfere with your duties. Aunt Malbot has suddenly had to come to London for some business matter that I don't begin to understand, but I'm sure that you would."

He made a lame-sounding response. Mrs. Malbot only nodded at him rather than attempting any consultation about financial matters. Not being in love, she was far more sensible in such a decision than her niece. After accepting Mr. Gardyne's greetings with some reserve, she followed the banker to his office.

As he watched them briefly, it crossed Arthur's mind that the banker could speak about this search for employment, but Mr. Gardyne might not necessarily add that Arthur was a complete novice in these matters. Because Vivien was so close, Arthur had the feeling that he would be lucky.

"I didn't have any idea that you are connected with Mr. Gardyne's establishment," she said amiably.

"I'm not. That is, not actually." Arthur wanted nothing more than to dally forever with his Vivien, as he thought of her. At the same time he recognized the importance to them both of his seeing the sinister-sounding Mr. Wolverstone as quickly as possible, and hopefully make certain of shortly being among the blessed in the field of commerce. "I must leave now."

"Don't you even want to know where you can reach me?" She took pity on his fresh embarrassment. "We are staying at Limmer's Hotel, as I am told most visitors do when they come up from the country. We arrived this morning and there has been no time to inform any local friends of their good fortune, so to speak."

"That's wonderful. I mean it is wonderful to see you in London." His eyes strayed to a point above Vivien's poke bonnet and the top of the outer door.

"I am sure that you are busy on some mission of importance," Vivien said with a sunny smile. "You must tell me eveything when we see each other again."

"Yes, yes."

"And you must arrange for my aunt at least to see you at work so that her suspicions about you can be stilled."

"Tonight, then. I mean tomorrow. Yes, you will certainly see me at work tomorrow."

"I must tell you something that will surely prove amusing. My Aunt Malbot still thinks that you are a parasite upon the fringes of civilization. That is how she referred to you in the train on the way down."

"Most amusing," Arthur said a little weakly.

He suddenly reached out for her hands and held them in his, drawing further resolution from their warmth. With a feeling that he had virtually torn himself away, he withdrew and hurried out to the street. Never would he have believed that it was possible for him to feel exalted and sad, happy and tense, at the same time. He was a young man who had accumulated considerable experience of the fair sex, but this was the only time he had ever been in love.

Bruton Street, to which he repaired in his quest for employment, lacked spaciousness to a more striking extent even than Cockspur Street, and made the latter seem, by comparison, as calm as the Dogs' Cemetery off the Bayswater Road in Hyde Park. The Wolverstone Bank was a two-story building no larger than William Royde's establishment, but without the saving grace that it generated continual interest.

His request for an interview with Mr. Derek Wolverstone was submitted to a clerk whose silver-rimmed spectacles, unlike Mr. Gardyne's, boasted square-shaped lenses. Style could be observed in financial quarters as well as in the civilized world, it appeared.

"Mr. Wolverstone, he won't be here for the balance of the day."

"Where can I find him?"

"He's at home, but surely isn't going to be available to visitors." Seeing that the gentleman before him was vexed and convinced that he might be of some importance, the clerk added, "Mr. W., he doesn't go home for his sleep every afternoon, but this is a special occasion. He wants to be shipshape-and-Bristol-fashion in case he has to wait up very late tonight."

"Some business matter to be transacted at an odd hour, I take it." Arthur ignored the clerk's skeptical chuckle and tried to put a casual note into his voice. "Will I be able to find him tonight at some public place, then, can you tell me?"

"I shouldn't ought to peach on Mr. W., indeed I shouldn't, sir." One more look at this visitor's expensive rig-out determined the clerk on a decision. "Mr. Wolverstone will be joining other young bloods of London tonight, for a rare change."

"What do you mean? Why?"

"As I understand it, there's a very unusual event to take

place at ten o'clock in one of the illegal gambling places, where two men will be going at it for one certain girl."

Arthur drew a deep pained breath. He could well believe that news of the matter had been transmitted everywhere, and as a result *le monde* was going to make an event of Royde's joust with Trevor for Camilla's hand. Not long ago he would have been first in line to observe the ructions if some other girl had been involed. Over this last week, however, he had developed what he considered a fine sense of delicacy, and the attitude of former friends in this matter would be appalling to him.

Certainly he hadn't planned on ever going near William Royde's gambling hell again, but Mr. Derek Wolverstone would be among the revelers on this night. It was clear to Arthur that a celebrated proverb ought to be amended to make the point that needs must when a banker drives.

CHAPTER EIGHTEEN

Camilla was sending Annie, the maid of most work, out to the phaeton to await her when there was an interruption. Blackhouse, the omnipotent butler of the Fairfield establishment, manifested himself in the door of the large sitting room.

"A young woman is anxious to see you, Miss Camilla."

"Ask her to return at another time."

"She will, I think, decline to do so, Miss Camilla. She is a most determined young woman."

"I have no time to spare, but you may tender my regrets."

Camilla spared one look at herself in the mirror. Her high-necked rose dress showed a good figure. As her brother had informed her over breakfast that Trevor kept lodgings in the Albany on the north side of Piccadilly, she was off to see him before the night's gaming. The visit would serve to assure Trevor once more of her deep devotion. She was not cake-wit enough to visit the House of Lords for that purpose, as she knew it was most unlikely to find a sensible peer in Parliament if no business of great national importance was to be transacted.

"There's no time to be lost," said Edith Jessop, making her entrance with a flair that would have caused Mrs. Sarah Siddons herself to nod admiringly.

In costume as well as words Edith was ready to make her presence felt. She wore a violet day dress under accessories in three colors, and her red hair had been tortured into showy ringlets.

Camilla heard a clucking of disapproval from Annie. Rather

than auditing a colloquy between the two, she sent her maid out. Blackhouse didn't seem surprised that Edith Jessop had disregarded instructions to wait and eased herself past the sitting room door as he had moved inside. Now the butler looked appraisingly at her, ready to act on whatever instructions Camilla might issue.

"That will be all, Blackhouse," Camilla said quietly. Because of the particular circumstances involving tonight's encounter, it could be wise to hear whatever William Royde's former inamorata had come to impart. The only proviso was that Edith Jessop not occupy too much time.

The visitor seemed more than willing to oblige, foregoing the chance to be seated.

"I've come to offer advice, and hope you'll take it," she began.

"I am surprised you would ever talk to me again," Camilla couldn't help saying.

"You mean because you couldn't convince Willie that you have no use for him?" Edith Jessop shrugged violently, the accessories on her costume performing a small dance as a result. "Willie, he has a head like a pint o' beer, sometimes."

"You have my apologies, then. Frankly, you may have gathered that I am presently in something of a hurry. Brevity from you—I intend no rudeness—would be deeply appreciated."

"Short is how you'll get it," Edith Jessop agreed. "I'm talking about this special and particular bit of gaming as is due to get done tonight."

Camilla nodded. Like her brother, she wasn't surprised that the matter had come to everyone's knowledge up and down London. Anybody attempting to keep a secret in *le monde* would have been pilloried for displaying a true affectation.

"The stakes are high and Willie is anxious to win, from what I hear. Very anxious." Edith Jessop's face reflected hurt, but not for long. "Ask me, and I'll say he's in a foul mood 'cause he hasn't been eating well."

Camilla blinked at what appeared to be a change of subject, then recalled that Edith Jessop considered herself a splendid cook and Royde had ousted her from his life, in part, because of a feeling that the capacity to cook well was beneath the dignity of a true lady. It was a response of which only a formerly poor man would have been capable.

"A man don't eat well, and his stomach gets so roiled up that he doesn't know what's best for him," Edith Jessop continued. "I don't mean that Willie eats bad if I'm not cooking for him, only that the food he takes aboard hasn't been prepared with his own personal quirks being considered. You can see, then, as how—yes, yes, I know!" One look at Camilla's drawn lips had reminded Edith Jessop of the need for urgency. "What I'm saying is that Willie considers as the doings tonight are very important to him."

"I accept that; perforce I must. But what other points do you wish to make as following from it?"

"Just that for once in his life Willie could be tempted to cheat. I haven't spoken to him in a while, but I know him well enough to be sure I'm right."

It was a consideration which had escaped Camilla's notice. All the same, a man who was capable of using such tactics as Royde had already done would at least be aware of the advantages to be gained by cheating at a game for the desirable stakes. And his opponent was a peer not as experienced in gaming as Royde.

"What is to be done?"

"You must visit your friend, what's-his-name, the Earl of Muckymuck—"

Camilla was so absorbed that she didn't offer any correction or show annoyance.

"—and say to him, 'Earl, you have to make sure that the only game you play with Willie Royde tonight is the game of faro.' That's what you have to say."

"But why must it be faro?"

"Because cheating at it is as near impossible as can be."

"Pardon me, but I find a difficulty believing that men who earn their bread and salt through gaming have not discovered a method to gain their objective in the course of a game of cards."

"Willie told me it's very unlikely anyone could cheat in faro, and he was a good friend of mine when he said it. I can recollect that he was just finishing a dish of my scalloped oysters when the subject came up."

Camilla found that testimony acceptable, considering the sources. Certainly it was worth acting upon at this critical juncture in her affairs.

Edith Jessop added a little defensively, "That's what I came to tell you. Now I'm going."

"I am obliged to you," Camilla said formally, although well aware that the information was going to help both of them if it could be acted upon.

Edith turned away, the accessories moving thunderously with her.

"May I keep you one moment longer?" Camilla asked. "I wish to offer a suggestion to you now."

"Oh? And what would that be?"

"For your own sake you ought to dress more plainly. Many females of a higher station in life do so nowadays. It is considered admirable to have financial resources, but not to flaunt that one fact before others."

Edith Jessop's head was pulled back, angry responses hovering on her lips. A moment's reflection showed that the suggestion had been well intended. She looked at Camilla indecisively, as if to thank her for a very real favor, but couldn't bring herself to get out the words in speaking to the female who had so powerfully attracted the man she loved. Nonetheless she turned slowly, as if to keep the accessories silent. She was making an acknowledgment without speech, and Camilla accepted it similarly.

Camilla found herself delighted by the sturdy Albany as soon as it came into her sight from the phaeton that Annie was driving. At some other time she would have looked around carefully, if not with greater pleasure.

Trevor's rooms were among those located along the covered passage that ran to Burlington Gardens. His door was opened by a thin young man who obviously served as a butler in the second establishment Trevor kept here.

"I wish to see the Duke."

A woman's voice from inside the anteroom called out, "Is that Miss Fairfield?"

The butler stood aside, permitting Camilla to walk in and Annie back of her. The Dowager Duchess of Strafford was in the room, having apparently descended on London from the family eyrie in Kent. She wore gray and white, a combination styled for the uncritical provinces but somehow looking handsome on her.

"I am in London for one of my quarterly visits," said the Dowager Duchess, leading Camilla into the comfortable room where paperfall stirred in the banked fireplace and gewgaws had been reduced to a minimum. "I have communicated these tidings to your family and hope to visit with them before leaving to resume my contented ways."

"You will be most welcome, I do assure you," Camilla murmured, though hard put to it to think of any situation but the one into which she had been thrust.

"I am hoping to persuade my son to act in his own best interests," the Dowager Duchess said, gesturing Camilla to a klismos-type chair that any resident of ancient Greece would have promptly disowned. "Trevor has brought it to my attention that tonight he will be gaming for the right to court you."

"And you disapprove of this?"

"As would any rational human being, yes," the Dowager Duchess added quietly. "No young man should have to game for the female with whom he wishes to make a life."

"But you've come to feel less wary at the possibility that Trevor and I might wed?" Camilla remembered their conversation at Strafford, in which the older woman had spoken of her trepidations in a forthright manner.

"I have indeed come to approve," the Dowager Duchess agreed. "After seeing you and Trevor together at home and listening to him speak on the subject of your attributes, my consent was sure to follow."

"For that I am grateful."

"The two of you appear to complement each other in many ways, and I cannot but imagine that you will be of help to him.

Trevor feels that he can always evolve some action so as to avoid the worst of any difficulty. For example, his lively dislike of husband-hunting in London caused him to conceive the stratagem into which he persuasively enticed you and therefore caused anguish to many people. This current experience, no matter how it is resolved, should teach him that stratagems are not always preferable to directness. That is, if he doesn't —" The Dowager Duchess took a deep breath. "At any rate, I am pleased that you have come here. Perhaps you can speak to him in a way that will seem to him to be sensible."

Camilla understood that mother and son had been embroiled in some disagreement stemming from the position in which he found himself. Her first impulse was to take Trevor's side, but about this feeling she was tactfully silent.

Trevor himself entered within the moment, making it clear why the Dowager Duchess had broken off her explanations of the quarrel that had arisen. He took two steps towards Camilla and she couldn't help standing to greet him. She felt warm and happy at being in his presence again.

"During my day," the Dowager Duchess said crisply, "chaperones were present but largely ignored. I find it gall and wormwood to be ignored and will happily withdraw if both of you give me your word that nothing will be done or said that would be out of place in Queen Vickie's presence."

"My word, Mother."

"And mine."

The Dowager Duchess took her leave.

Trevor, about to embrace Camilla, pulled back reluctantly. "The Queen might not possibly give her wholehearted approval to such a maneuver."

"Surely she would," Camilla said, deciding that her previous strictures against the monarch, those complaints of a girl unattached, had been much too harsh. "Nonetheless, in the spirit of our agreement with your dear mother, we must defer the pleasure."

"Reluctantly."

"Most reluctantly," Camilla agreed. "It occurs to me that we could be done with familial obligations and other difficulties if the two of us leave England and take ourselves off to one of the colonies."

"Such as Australia, you mean? But it reeks of convicts, as I understand matters, and I would worry about you every moment you were away."

"We could migrate to a province in America."

"I would not feel contented in a nation whose residents had rebelled against my native land." He shook his head. "It should not be necessary to graft ourselves away from the settings we know and love."

"Indeed it *should* not." Camilla raised the second alternative. "One more possibility has been brought to my attention if we remain. It is not without a flaw, but offers us a fair chance at the happiness we crave."

In the fewest possible words she told about Edith Jessop's recent visit to Lower Brook Street and offered the advice that had been given.

"Cheating at faro is nearly impossible, Trevor, as I understand it. Therefore you have to insist that you and Royde game only at faro."

She would have expected Trevor to agree immediately. Instead he turned towards the curtained window and frowned.

"Will Royde isn't known to be dishonest, nor have I been told of cheating in his establishment," Trevor said carefully. "I cannot believe that Royde would indulge in or condone any behavior along that line."

"He is a villain! Have you already forgotten what was done by his men to my brother?"

"I venture to disagree on that implicit point, Camilla. If Arthur hadn't become irritable, those messengers of Royde would have spoken briefly to me and disappeared back into the smoke from which they came."

"In other words, my brother having sustained an injury from a fist was entirely his own fault." Camilla flushed. "Is that how you feel?"

"Substantially, yes. Arthur would concede the point in a quiet conversation between us. We can all, including Royde himself, be thankful that no lasting harm was done."

She had not expected that the talk would follow this particular path, like a dropped stitch that causes numberless diversions in its train. Nor was there time to discuss the family's grievances against anyone who had done Arthur the least disservice.

"In dealing with someone like Royde, it is necessary to take precautions against any adverse development," she pointed out, marshaling logic to her side. "It is possible that Royde may consider cheating and you must react in such a way that any attempt he makes along such a line will be ineffective."

"No action of his in that direction would be of any significance against me."

"What can you possibly mean by that?"

He hesitated. "I wish you wouldn't be so persistent in this matter."

"I must, Trevor, for your sake as well as mine."

"In that case, I may tell you (in confidence, to be sure) that I strongly anticipate a favorable outcome to this night's gaming."

A flash of understanding made it clear to her what he actually meant. Nor was it difficult now to realize exactly what Trevor and his mother, the Dowager Duchess, had quarreled about earlier in the day.

She whispered, "Are you telling me that *you* plan to cheat?"

Trevor drew himself up. For a man who was so adroit at drawing the proper inferences when listening to others, it was a surprise to him that similar treatment from another was leaving him in a state close to simmering resentment.

"I say only that I will be very surprised indeed if I lose."

She wanted to add that he wasn't speaking of what the two of them would feel when it became known that he had attempted to cheat. The action itself was horrendous to contemplate. As it was to be made against a man who actually dealt in gaming for his sole income, the likelihood of being detected was very high. Trevor's prospects in London, perhaps as a durable cog in governing the Empire, would be smashed irrevocably. On social terms Trevor and his wife would become outcasts. Camilla was capable of living with a man under those terms as she truly loved him, but the scandal was entirely unnecessary.

"I plan to make absolutely sure that there will be no question of the outcome," he added.

She couldn't bring herself to point out drily that he also expected to be gaining pleasure from the stratagem, from outwitting another. Clearly he wasn't able to accept the thought that his actions could hurt both of them forever.

"No matter what you say, Camilla, my mind won't be changed about this," he added, probably in the same tone with which he had recently addressed his mother.

Camilla knew the strength of his resolution. She wouldn't have considered it possible to turn away from him at any time, but she did it now.

Softly he spoke after her. "Aren't you going to wish me well?"

"I could never wish you anything else," she answered, not raising her voice either.

She turned back for one quick look at the man with whom she had fallen deeply in love, and then hurried out.

CHAPTER NINETEEN

Between Vivien and her Aunt Malbot, on this afternoon of their London visit, tempers had also been running high. The older woman was initially outraged by Mr. Gardyne, the banker, after her brief *causerie* in his lair. The difficulty was one that Vivien couldn't bring herself to comprehend in full despite her aunt's explanations. Her mind was wholly occupied elsewhere.

Shortly after leaving the banker's presence, as a result, Mrs. Malbot was subjected to demands from her niece.

Vivien had become determined to make a call upon the Fairfields of Lower Brook Street and leave a card if none of the family was available for being visited. It was useless for the older woman to protest that she herself and Lady Fairfield had reached an uneasy truce in the country and cared for each other not at all. Vivien pointed out that as *she* had every intention of marrying that distinguished young man of business, Arthur Fairfield, a *modus operandi* between the older women should be evolved as a matter of course.

The Widow Malbot eventually grew weary of continuing the discussion and acceded to her niece's request, certain that Nora, Lady Fairfeld, would take pains to inform the butler that she wasn't at home. In this the Widow Malbot made an error. Lady Fairfield, having previously decided against impeding the already difficult path to marriage that was facing her son, asked the females to enter the large sitting room and made much of Vivien.

A worried Camilla, arriving home in the middle of the afternoon, nonetheless embraced the other girl with enthusiasm. It seemed to her that the difference between the two maidens was simply that Vivien was wholly unaware of the obstacle to her wedding, while Camilla could have enumerated the various problems in her own case on each individual finger of both hands.

Arthur, weary and tense at the same time, returned home towards the end of the afternoon. For once the sight of Vivien perked him up only briefly.

"You must've had a difficult day," Vivien began, resuming her efforts to persuade Aunt Malbot of Arthur's importance in the great world of finance. To Lady Fairfield she added, "We saw him today, and he was too occupied to say a word to my aunt or me. At Mr. Gardyne's bank, it was."

Mrs. Malbot didn't object to Vivien's assessment of the young man, partly because she was seething at mention of Mr. Gardyne and his establishment. Any firm expression of her feelings, however, was kept to herself.

Arthur made a noncommittal rejoinder.

"Tell my aunt about it," Vivien requested, pride in his undoubted achievement giving a glow to her voice.

That was too much for Mrs. Malbot. "Even if the young man is employed in some area of one of those pirate ships as a first mate or even a cook, and could put down his cutlass long enough to support you and a family, I have no wish to hear about his depredations against innocent country women."

"Aunt Malbot had a diffcult interview with Mr. Gardyne on account of some bonds, as I understand it." Vivien was again struck by a thought that seemed severely practical. "Perhaps you, Mr. Fairfield, as a colleague of Mr. Gardyne's and therefore knowledgeable in these matters, perhaps you could intervene with him and put matters right."

Camilla, as an auditor, did not laugh. It would have been impossible to make such a response to a young lady speaking with palpable sincerity and great affection.

Arthur couldn't help jumping slightly, reminding his sister of a horse which has received a communication urging it to move with greater celerity.

Lady Fairfield, aware of the dimensions of her son's difficulty, serenely rescued him. "Before you ladies depart from
London, I feel sure that Arthur will consent to be of service."

Further discussion of her son's wisdom in financial matters
was cut short by Sir Osric's arrival. The diplomat had spent an
afternoon at the Lollard Club, one of the numerous social
organizations to which he belonged. Having shrewdly returned from the Lambeth Palace area just before supper, he
found himself subjected to very little conversation from the
visiting females and none whatever from his wife and daughter. As for Arthur, he was content to stare at Vivien in silent
wonder.

Arthur didn't stir himself until after supper, a meal which
Edith Jessop herself, having cooked her way into William
Royde's regard, would have proudly created. When the last
dollop of flanc meringue had been washed down with the last
cup of steaming Lapsang souchong, he got to his feet with
great reluctance.

"I must leave now."

Vivien's features reflected his own keen disappointment.
"Must you go?"

"Yes. Oh, yes." He swallowed. Under no circumstances
would he admit that he was on his way to a gambling hell, if
only so that he could meet a banker who might quickly offer
employment to him.

"It must be a matter of business, I'm sure," Vivien said.

"Nothing else would tear me away," Arthur told her, stat-
ing a fact and evading the truth with a skill worthy of Sir Osric.

Mrs. Malbot cocked her head sharply. "Business? At a time
when affluent London is at ease?"

Vivien said a little severely, "To a man of business there are
few opportunities for untrammeled relaxation."

Mrs. Malbot continued to look doubtful, but realized she
had already exposed herself to a charge of bad manners by
speaking unfavorably of Arthur while a visitor at the home of
his parents.

"I suppose that's true," she said too loudly, apologizing
indirectly and yet again after an offense had been given.

Arthur, in spite of his discomfort, observed that Mrs. Malbot appeared hostile towards men of business as such. It seemed that he was exerting himself to reach a position in life of which Vivien's aunt would not approve, but even Mrs. Malbot was bound to realize that he would amply provide for Vivien. The older woman's attitude was an added irritation, and only his love for Vivien would have caused him to tolerate conditions that he would never before have accepted.

With the son of the house proceeding on his way, there was no reason for these visitors to linger. Mrs. Malbot waited half an hour before notifying her hosts that she and Vivien would soon be leaving. She added, in the course of conversation, that in two days at a minimum they would be returning to Kent, gratefully on her own part. With expressions of regard among the ladies and oft-used courtesy from the bland Sir Osric, they took their departure.

Vivien waited until the infallible Blackhouse had put her and Mrs. Malbot into a cab, then adverted to the subject of the recent disagreement between them.

"Arthur would not have left so quickly," she insisted, "if a matter of business wasn't involved."

"He doesn't have the callousness for a true man of business," Mrs. Malbot insisted, only preventing herself at the last minute from adding a snort to emphasize her feelings. "I approve far less of a parasite than I do of a businessman, although my experience with Mr. Gardyne has finally convinced me that the distinction is a more narrow one than I had previously suspected."

"Why did Arthur leave us earlier, then, in your jaundiced view?"

"To disport himself, I feel sure," Mrs. Malbot said, nodding firmly. "If you discover the most popular place of bad repute in London—I do not say ill repute, necessarily, with all its connotations—there you will find Arthur Fairfield in his element tonight."

"I cannot accept a word of that."

"No, my dear, you *will* not accept it."

The temper that was connoted by Vivien's red hair suddenly came to the surface because of what she considered an injustice.

"That is not true, Aunt Malbot!"

"Neither of us can prove it," Mrs. Malbot said, withdrawing only slightly because of the prospect of acrimonious discussion. "The point doesn't arise."

"I demand that we make an attempt to prove it," Vivien said briskly, raising her head and voice. "Driver!"

That worthy's face appeared where a closed panel had previously been plain.

"Driver, what would you say is the most popular place of amusement in the city at this time of a weeknight?"

"Miss?" The driver blinked.

"You heard me, I feel sure!"

The driver, whose name was Herbert Elkott, rubbed a gloved hand against his brow, displacing the traditional curly-brimmed top hat of the sort which was favored by his colleagues. He was used to queries along that line, but not from females.

"I'm not sure exactly what you ladies would have in mind," he began.

Mrs. Malbot, flushing to the roots of her hair, turned impatiently to Vivien. "There is no way to agree on the single most popular den of iniquity in this city, and it is therefore entirely possible that young Fairfield would perversely patronize one of the lesser-known places. I concede that much. Can we now either discuss some other aspect of life or fall blessedly silent?"

Vivien shook her head at Aunt Malbot, then held the driver's watery eyes with her own.

"I want no information more or less than I have already requested."

"Well, now, I have to think on that." The driver paused to negotiate a difficult street maneuver with his pair of horses. "Usually I wouldn't be able to offer but one place out of six, and it's odds on that you wouldn't be permitted inside—you two ladies don't exactly seem like London sparrows."

"We are not," Mrs. Malbot agreed firmly, not caring if an inferior's sensibilities were ruffled by the emphasis.

"Tonight, though, is a little different," the driver continued imperturbably. "I think I can be of some use. There's a place in the city where a very unusual gambling game will be going on. As I understand it, Billy Royde is playing someone else for the right to marry the girl he fancies."

"That is barbaric," Mrs. Malbot snapped. "Does this sort of jousting occur very often?"

"First time I ever heard of anything like it," the driver said. "Every blood in the city should be on the scene, and I'm sure it'll be easy to slip into the place as you're dressed in a refined way in that crowd. Billy Royde is located on Bennet Street, not far away at all."

The driver sounded encouraging. As it happened, Royde's place was a little farther off than Limmer's Hotel, and a greater charge for the transportation would be justified. The ladies, of course, couldn't possibly know that.

"I see no reason for us venturing into such an Augean stable as this man hints at," Mrs. Malbot said.

"I do, Aunt. It will prove what I have been saying if much of London's young society is at the scene and Arthur has been called elsewhere to transact some business," Vivien pointed out by way of rebuttal. "Driver, take us to this gambling hell immediately!"

Camilla, running upstairs, did not know that her brother and the Malbot females would soon be on the premises of William Royde's flourishing enterprise. Her own reason for wanting to attend was at least as strong as theirs. She remained anxious to be sure that only the almost cheat-proof card game of faro was played by the contenders for her hand. No other way of doing so was available to her, except that of insisting on it before witnesses at the event.

Never had she reached more quickly for a dark cloak to cover the pale yellow crinoline she was wearing. Never had she paused so briefly to inspect herself in the cheval glass. Automatically she tamped down a straying segment of bright blond hair and then reached, as an afterthought, for a small muslin indoors bonnet.

She was in the throes of leaving when Mamma suddenly entered. Lady Fairfield had been attracted by the unexpected sounds issuing from this room. For the first time she discovered her daughter setting out on a nocturnal expedition.

Rather than criticizing Camilla for making unauthorized forays into the City, Lady Fairfield addressed herself to another aspect of the matter.

"You mustn't go out to that place!"

Camilla spoke quietly, which neither she nor Lady Fairfield probably realized was a great compliment in this circumstance. "I must make sure that faro is played, and no other game. That way cheating can almost certainly be prevented."

Perhaps, if she'd felt there was more time, Camilla might have added that it was necessary to avert skulduggery by Trevor as well as by the odious William Royde.

Lady Fairfield considered. It went against her every feeling to permit the girl to leave, but any other action at this time would be eternally unforgivable.

"Camilla, would you want me to accompany you?"

The daughter took grateful notice that it was her full given name being used rather than the trivializing contraction that the older woman generally favored.

"Thank you, no. Thank you very much, but no."

Camilla had sensed that she would lack for any necessary freedom of action if a decision of hers needed to be justified to an older woman. It was a point which Vivien Malbot, condemned to her aunt's company for the better part of this important night, would have heartily endorsed.

"Do you want your father to go with you?" Lady Fairfield asked.

It was a temptation, as the diplomatist was reputed to be skillful in the swaying of forces in contention. No less a personage than Charles the Fourteenth of Sweden and Norway had spoken favorably of him in public. It was known that Prince Alexander Karageorgevich had praised Sir Osric's ability during a speech before the Serbian Diet. Sir Osric was not a man whose gifts had gone unrecognized beyond his hearth.

Camilla still didn't want to be in the position of deferring to another, and Sir Osric's influence over these gamesters would not be nearly as great as Camilla's own. Most important of all, she needed to be the one who made certain choices. No one else must be responsible for efforts made in her behalf.

"I have to leave now," she said, and paused long enough to kiss her mother warmly on the cheek.

Lady Fairfield, left in the room, considered that her daughter's second expression of good feeling in several days, although given in return for her own, was nevertheless deeply moving.

CHAPTER TWENTY

It has previously been pointed out that the suitable description of chaotic events requires a pen wielded by genius. Even the most gifted of chroniclers, however, another Mrs. Gaskell or, to scale the very heights of literary composition, Mrs. Humphrey Ward herself, might be daunted in making an attempt to describe the scene on Bennet Street shortly before ten o'clock that night.

The street was chockablock with young men in formal dress, each insisting on admittance to the temple of chance that was owned and managed by Will Royde. Confronting these men, and a number of women, were an orderly and three others with whom Arthur was familiar, to his cost.

Arthur, having arrived before the other principal characters of this tale, waded through the crowd in hopes of reaching one of the four guardians of the portals. Participants were making complicated wagers on the outcome of the night's sporting event. Arthur smiled and waved at friends not far off. Even Lord George Bentinck, that celebrated gambler, deflected for once from his vocation of muddling the course of empire, had come to see the doings and was unable to gain admission.

"I've gambled for clothing and furniture, and once for a streetlamp," Lord George admitted to Arthur, making his voice heard over the uproar, "but never for a wife. Perhaps I have been remiss."

Arthur gestured that he was keenly sympathetic to Lord George's feelings, whatever those might be, and moved on.

Progress was slower as he reached the guardians, who were shouting at the nearest gamblers and had linked arms to keep the distinguished patrons from entering.

Arthur knew one of these Charons. It was the toothless man who had made such a sterling effort to relocate Arthur's jaw in line with the back of his neck.

"You!" He remembered the man's name as Royde had given it in the course of the recent four-sided conversation in the National Gallery. "Here you! Ernie!"

The miscreant jumped at hearing his name spoken by one of the gentlemen. A squint of the eyes permitted him to discern Arthur and wince at the recollection of their former meeting.

"I have to talk to Billy Royde," Arthur shouted. "Get him for me!"

"I can't move from here."

"You owe me a favor, Ernie, after what you did," Arthur pointed out censoriously. "Billy Royde will appreciate it, too."

The combination of arguments swayed the reluctant Ernie, who had probably been rated by his employer after the fracas near the premises. "You come in and wait just by the door. I'll get him to you."

The maneuvering required was far from simple, but both men accomplished it. In a brief time Arthur found himself standing on the other side of the door. He felt galvanized by the certainty that Mr. Derek Wolverstone, the banker who might offer employment and solve his difficulties with Vivien and her aunt, was nearby. To find him quickly he had to get help, and Billy Royde was most likely to provide it in return for another favor.

Royde was scowling ferociously as he descended the stairs. Arthur, watching the dark-haired, beetle-browed impresario of gambling advance on him, decided that the man was sinister-looking, which he had never before noticed. Edith Jessop, if she had seen her former friend at that moment, would have recognized the particular malaise as stemming from ill-cooked viands which had been digested not long ago.

"Do you know what's happening outside?" Arthur began.

Royde cocked his head. "It sounds like Bagnigge Wells on a Saturday night, almost." He gritted his teeth. "Whoever put the word of this night's doings about ought to be boiled in oil at the very least."

"Most likely you were too upset to realize just how bad it was until I asked you to come down," Arthur said. "Think it over and you will agree that it is wiser to have your employees let in people known in the establishment."

An effort at judicial consideration was almost beyond Royde's present powers in light of the internal turbulence at his midriff.

"I will not," he began loudly, then dropped a palm to rub himself in the afflicted area. Such results as he obtained were enough to cause him to lower his voice and consider the fresh difficulty. "If so much noise gets made out there, the peelers will be coming up soon enough and they'll take everybody to the pokey."

"Exactly."

Royde's eyes narrowed suspiciously. "I suppose you've warned me because you want to get inside as the brother of the girl I will be contending for as soon as that infernal Strafford gets here. You want to disturb the game."

"I give my word that I won't." Nothing that Arthur might do could keep the encounter from taking place.

"You want something in return, I'm blurry sure."

"I would like you or somebody else to point Mr. Derek Wolverstone out to me as soon as he enters."

"The banker?" Royde shrugged. "All right, cully. You scratched my back, now I do yours. I'll talk to one of my waiters and he'll handle it for you."

Arthur felt so exhausted that he refrained for once from politely expressing his gratitude.

Vivien and her aunt endured their next painful surprise as soon as they dismounted from the cab and looked out at the well-dressed throng. Vivien, her eyes sharpened by youth, saw the figure speaking to one of the guardians before the building.

"Is it Arthur?" she asked her aunt, who was unable to answer. Calling out would have been useless. The figure disappeared within even as she tried to make sure of his identity.

She said hoarsely, "It must be somebody who looks like Arthur."

"You don't really believe that," her Aunt Malbot charged, correctly in this case.

"I want to make absolutely certain Arthur is guilty of this—this perfidy."

"You would be better to leave such an infernal community as this one without a word and never write to Arthur Fairfield," Aunt Malbot insisted. "Any man who could marry you and declines to avail himself of the opportunity deserves not a whit better."

Vivien spared only the vaguest smile in acknowledgment of that kindly speech, then squeezed her aunt's hand in silent regard.

"No one else is being let in, so perhaps there isn't any choice about—no, I am wrong."

Mrs. Malbot, too, had seen that much. Men were being selectively admitted, and several women as well.

"I refuse to enter a—a financial establishment manqué," Mrs. Malbot said, once again recollecting her vivid encounter with Mr. Gardyne over a matter of bonds.

Vivien, undismayed, pressed forward.

"But I will not let you go in alone," Mrs. Malbot decided immediately.

She followed a pace back of Vivien in the crush. Men on the sidewalk were pausing to confirm wagers that had been previously made and add conditions and qualifiers. As a result she was able to move ahead swiftly.

The guard she confronted, a burly fellow with at least one gleaming gold tooth, shook his head decisively at her request.

"You can't get in, miss," he said. "You're not known."

It was Mrs. Malbot, wise in the world's ways to some extent, who settled the matter.

"We are friends of Mr. Arthur Fairfield," she said with a glance over at Vivien. "That should be sufficient confirmation of our *bona fides.*"

An equally burly guard, whose lack of teeth made it difficult for the ladies to understand his first words, interfered.

"Best to let 'em in," the toothless one said shortly. "Mr. Fairfield is the white-'aired bloke around 'ere tonight."

" 'Im? Well, if you say so, but it's not goin' to be on my 'ead if His Billyship is upset."

With that much agreed upon he drew back, permitting the newcomers to enter.

By this time Arthur had been approached by one of the waiters and told to follow him upstairs, a feat which he performed with alacrity.

The two gambling rooms were so crowded that men and women were standing almost shoulder-to-shoulder. Royde, at the farthest table, had accomplished the feat of looking more irritable than previously. Space had been cleared, permitting him to be seated. The chair that faced him at this table was unoccupied. The Duke of Strafford had not yet arrived to gamble for Camilla's hand.

The waiter, an older man with powerful shoulders like a boxer's, said, "Third man from the left, the smiling one, he's the one you want."

Arthur nodded. Derek Wolverstone—for that must be the other's identity—was young and seemed calm. Nor was he speaking with anyone, which meant that no conversation would have to be interrupted.

Aware of a brief commotion at the entrance and certain that Trevor had at last come, Arthur turned his head. He was in time to meet the scalding eyes of Vivien and then the icy ones of Mrs. Malbot. A gasp issued from between his lips.

Arthur looked away immediately, convinced that it would require several minutes of pushing, shoving, and apologizing to others before Vivien and her aunt could reach him. In that time he ought to have been able to approach Derek Wolverstone and whisper that he urgently required the banker to pose as his employer. Mr. Wolverstone, who looked like a pleasant and agreeable young man, must certainly be willing to oblige a fellow patron of Royde's.

To evolve this scheme took less time than putting it into action. Arthur moved towards the man who had been pointed out, approaching directly. At no time did he look over his shoulder to determine the progress of Vivien and her aunt. It made his behavior seem more natural and he would later be able to tell the ladies how surprised he was to confirm his impression of having seen them here.

"Excuse me," he whispered to Mr. Wolverstone. "I need a favor and you're the only one I know of in this room who can help me."

Although he was standing in front of the stranger and speaking clearly, Derek Wolverstone hadn't turned his head back from the left, having previously been distracted by some motion.

Arthur continued urgently, "When the two females coming over are nearer, you must speak to me as if I am an employee in your bank, Mr. Wolverstone. I ask this as a fellow sports-man, and I am sure that you will not fail me."

The banker's manner offered little reason for such sunny self-confidence on Arthur's part. Mr. Wolverstone was watch-ing the women approach determinedly and hadn't yet looked around towards the supplicant.

Discarding his good manners for this occasion, Arthur took several steps to the right so that he would be standing in front of the insensitive banker. He hoped that there was a look of easy confidence on his features and that they didn't reflect the desperation he was starting to feel.

In a stentorian voice the banker suddenly said, "Please stand out of my way, sir."

Arthur hardly heard Will Royde, at the far table, smack a hand against it for silence, nor did he hear Royde's outraged tone at this lapse in decorum. For once Arthur's temper got the best of him.

"Confound it, sir, can't you at least indicate that you heard what I said?"

"How is that?" The voice would have shaken the walls of Jericho. "What are you saying?"

There was a minor eruption from Royde once again.

Arthur paid no attention to that. He had originally spoken with great clarity, which caused him to realize that he had made a wholly unexpected bad choice of genie to solve his difficulty. As the females stopped less than a foot away and glowered, he was wondering almost distractedly how the banker was able to do business despite his disability, and supposed that there must be some invaluable cohort of his at the Wolverstone Bank. For Mr. Derek Wolverstone, the man who Arthur had hoped to convince quietly and promptly to offer the assistance needed so that he could retain the affection of Vivien, Mr. Derek Wolverstone happened to be as deaf as a post.

CHAPTER TWENTY-ONE

Camilla arrived as the crowd in front of Royde's had thinned out. Unaware of the previous turmoil, she received a hint of it at sight of four men in front of the entrance. The orderly, who knew her at least as a patron, courteously stepped to one side.

Camilla was aware of the presence of a crowd within from the moment she reached the hallway, and didn't know if she ought to feel disgusted or amused. None of her close acquaintances was in sight. The usual attendant busily stowed cloaks and capes in the anteroom. There was a co-worker with her on this occasion, but Camilla only saw that one from the back.

The first attendant, having deftly taken Camilla's cloak, remembered her. "What color mask this time, miss?"

"Nothing unusual tonight, if you please. Black or white will do."

The other attendant turned at the sound of her voice, and Camilla was looking in astonishment at no less important a cast member than Edith Jessop. The reluctantly discarded but still hopeful friend of William Royde put a finger to her lips in urging Camilla to remain unsurprised in appearance. As Camilla ventured toward the stairs, the buxom Edith followed and spoke quietly, answering the question she must have felt sure that Camilla wanted to ask.

"Everybody who works for Willie knows me, and when it was clear that people would be attending in quantity and I was outside, it was only sensible that I should be asked to help."

Camilla judged by the murmuring in the gambling rooms that the *pas de deux* hadn't got under way as yet. A moment's further curiosity could be indulged. "But why did you come at all?"

"I wanted to know what happens in the game," Edith said simply, adding, "The Duke has just gone upstairs."

Camilla's heart was beating a little faster.

Edith said calmly, "I wouldn't be able to get up by myself and be admitted, but in your company it'll be easier. You're a patron."

Camilla was disabused of the vagrant notion that Edith had joined her by the stairway to do nothing but satisfy her curiosity. Edith was obviously determined to gain admittance to the gambling rooms.

"At the very least I am a patron, yes," Camilla agreed, briefly irresolute.

Her decision was made by the confirmation that Edith was dressed more sensibly than Camilla had ever seen her in the past, which proved that good advice about her appearance had been accepted. Being seen with Edith in this guise wouldn't cause any embarrassment.

"I see nothing to be gained by lurking on the outer edges," Camilla said. The witnesses in the rooms upstairs were becoming quieter. "Shall we attack the fortress?"

And Edith answered realistically, "Let's us go upstairs."

"Yes, 'let's us,' by all means."

Camilla was startled at the first sight of these familiar gambling rooms on this particular night. Waiters stood against the walls rather than hurrying to serve patrons. Many tables had been cleared away. Men waited in irregular rows to see what would be happening. Women looked ill at ease, and nearly all were masked. The smell of tobacco, jarring to Camilla's senses in the past, was completely absent.

At her brief imperious gesture a waiter who recalled her was quick to stifle his protest at Edith coming in.

From the corner of her eye she noticed that Arthur stood ill at ease although silent, and that Vivien and Mrs. Malbot were nearby. It struck Camilla that her brother had chosen an unusual entertainment with which to regale a pair of ladies from the provinces, having probably made the arrangement with Vivien before she officially left Lower Brook Street. Camilla didn't feel particularly surprised at Arthur's presence as a witness of this special brangle.

She moved forward, not knowing or caring if Edith was close by. Several steps caused her to make up her mind that it would be more convenient to go around a side. Other patrons made room for her, which they would almost certainly have scorned to do for a man.

In the nearest row she managed to get her first view of the battlefield to come. Each contestant was sitting at an oblong table with one raised wooden side and facing the other. The sight of Trevor caused her to feel vitalized, as ever. There was a glint of amusement in those unforgettable nile green eyes, and a quirk to his lips.

Royde, glancing across at him, looked unsettled. The man must have been irritated by the crowd which had forced its presence onto the scene, and in alliance with his opponent's air of patrician drollery it was galling to him. Illuminated by candles in varicolored glass containers, his skin looked sallow.

Trevor may have felt Camilla's eyes on him. He looked up. She knew she had been recognized in spite of the mask, but he seemed wary instead of being cheered by her presence.

It was Will Royde who looked encouraged, ducking his head in her direction. He probably felt that she had shown her approval of this means of settling the dispute between himself and Trevor. Camilla, to be sure, was far from pleased.

Freshly stung by her attitude, Royde turned away. His head became rigid. With a crooking forefinger he signaled one of the waiters to him and whispered discreetly.

There was a pause, and then that waiter appeared close to Camilla but deeply in conversation with Edith. Royde's former friend nodded heavily and walked off and out of the room. No doubt Royde, because of that snobbishness he didn't share with most of his patrons, had decided that Edith wasn't in the proper class to be an unoccupied spectator at this occasion.

"Do you choose to play hazard?" Camilla asked, stirring

everyone because she spoke loudly. "A roll of seven or eleven will permit the first contestant who reaches it to keep the dice, and his succeeding roll will give him a point to make, but he loses if a seven appears before he can repeat the point. And on the basis of one player keeping the dice, the course of two lives will be determined."

Will Royde, who had started to his feet and drawn a palm towards the dice that were being put down between both men, suddenly halted.

Someone started muttering in restrained agreement with that point of view, but didn't speak more loudly.

A masked woman was under no compunction along those lines, and promptly raised her voice. "There has to be a certainty that the game has been played in as honest a manner as possible."

Royde's complexion was scarlet at the crystal clear suggestion that he would connive at cheating. He was unable to speak.

Trevor, having his own strategy for the game, defended this opponent. "I feel certain that Mr. Royde is an honest man."

A quarrel broke out among several patrons, most of whom espoused Will Royde's honesty.

Royde suddenly called out the name of that waiter who had certainly just been instructed by a gesture to eject Camilla. He shook his head. It was no time for passions to be inflamed still further.

Camilla said, "I am not disputing Mr. Royde's honesty. What I am insisting upon is that the game be one in which no one's honesty could possibly be questioned."

Somebody said, "It is possible to manipulate cards, too, as you must be aware."

"A predetermined conclusion is more difficult at faro than any other game," she insisted.

There was a pause. Trevor sat back, silent. Royde was so angry he couldn't bring himself to say a word or make a move.

A woman shouted, "Faro! It must be faro!"

A man called out, "We insist!"

Words trembled on Royde's lips. No doubt he would have

bitterly pointed out that no one had requested the presence of these witnesses, and that they had been admitted only to keep away any peelers attracted by street noises. Certainly he would have added regrets that he had arranged for this special game to be played on his premises, although it was the most logical of locations that could have been sought.

As he wasn't a fool, Royde was well aware now that his options were limited. For the sake of his reputation he had to follow the suggestion of his masked Lady Fortune. It meant the acceptance of a condition that had been set because of a bystander, even though that person had a particular interest in the outcome.

This time he turned pointedly to the nearest waiter and spoke loudly.

"Bring a fresh pack of cards," said Will Royde, behaving as if the defeat had only caused him to make a magnanimous concession. "The Duke and I shall be gaming at faro."

"Neither my opponent nor I," Royde said sonorously when an unopened deck of cards had been put down at a point midway between them, "should be able to touch those pasteboards that aren't given to us."

Trevor nodded after the briefest of pauses. "Given the situation as it now stands, there has to be a dealer."

The same masked woman who had previously called out to them was prepared with another suggestion. "The girl herself! Let it be the girl herself!"

Camilla's first instinct was to draw back. She didn't want to be under close inspection by so many witnesses. Soon enough she told herself that there was an even more important reason for not helping to determine her future. Keeping a distance now would give her the chance to claim afterwards that the results had been arrived at through no doing of hers whatever. If she followed the anonymous woman's well-meant suggestion, she would find herself under more pressure to admit that the way of settling this special dispute was valid. Not abiding by the results, then, would seem worse than simply unreasonable. It would be unsportsmanlike, which was the deadliest of social sins.

Royde, looking directly at Camilla, turned away and shook his head.

"Absolutely not!"

A murmur of disapproval went up from the crowd of men and women who were patrons of the establishment.

"It wouldn't be seemly to ask Miss—the young lady," Royde said, unsuccessfully hiding the disapproval he plainly felt.

He must have known perfectly well that she wouldn't be able to cheat in anyone's favor. The censoriousness etched on his features made it clear that he considered a female in Camilla's station to be above comporting herself publicly in such a manner if she was to become his wife. To a man like Royde, having matured in shabby-genteel surroundings at best, such apparently frivolous behavior must be considered unladylike.

There was a scattering of applause among onlookers, none from females.

"A woman should take part in what is happening here," one lady insisted.

"Especially that particular woman," said another, a female who had almost certainly recognized Camilla in spite of the mask.

It seemed that more than one of the patrons might know her, and the others would certainly hear about her presence tonight. No longer did it matter from that point of view if she participated or not. As for the other objection, it could be nullified, in great part, if this example of Royde's snobbishness pervaded other aspects of his thinking as well. Once he realized that the woman he wanted to marry was someone of an independent turn of mind, he was likely to consider carefully before committing himself further, no matter what the results of this gaming session.

"I would be honored by a chance to take a role in these revels," she said clearly.

There was another burst of applause, not only from many

of the assembled females but from a number of the men as well.

"No, it isn't," Royde began, and then swallowed. "It shouldn't be—" He was unable to speak further, so affronted did he plainly feel. Never before could he have been so completely at a loss.

Camilla was already moving forward.

CHAPTER TWENTY-TWO

Greater applause followed as Camilla approached the gambling table. It occurred to her, waspishly perhaps, that no patrons could have more eagerly anticipated the entrance of an unarmed early Christian into an arena to face a lion.

She circled the table, giving Royde a wide berth. Standing behind the white-wrapped package of playing cards, she held it firmly by one hand while easing a thumbnail under the seal and lifting slightly. The package was torn. Cards appeared, white-backed, as were all pasteboards.

Trevor, speaking because Royde remained too indignant, said, "Shuffle the cards, please."

She did so, carefully keeping her hands open when she was done as a way of showing beyond dispute that she hadn't removed any of the pasteboards.

Trevor, sounding calm as ever, said, "Please give the card on top to me, face up."

She did, setting it before him. As he wasn't in a direct line, she was unable to discern which suit he had received and she didn't want to make a point of looking further in that direction. Someone had told her that there was talk of manufacturing double-headed playing cards so that the suit, at least, could have been identified from the location in which she found herself. That improvement, if such it was, would be coming along too late to solve her difficulties.

"Please give the next card, also face up, to my opponent."

This she did also, more quickly, and not troubling herself to think of discovering the suit of which Royde had been dealt a representative. No expression whatever enlivened the man's features.

"Please call out the rank of the next card you put down."

"Clubs." She added unnecessarily, "The three of clubs."

Trevor looked relieved. A club wasn't either man's suit or both would have lost. Royde made no move, but his eyes seemed narrowed.

"Do the same with the next card, but deposit this one at your right."

She did, and said, "Six of diamonds."

Trevor hadn't stirred this time. Royde remained motionless. If either man had been dealt a club or diamond, that one would have been the victor. Had each man been dealt a different card of the same suit, she took it for granted that the whole grisly charade would be starting up again. There seemed no other way to ensure the maximum of honesty, but the sensibilities of even the strongest onlooker were bound to be severely frayed.

"One card at the left again this time," Trevor instructed politely.

Another club.

Trevor ventured on a pleasantry. " 'Pon my word, I think that we are going to exhaust every club and diamond as well before getting to the other ranks."

The next card seemed to be bearing out his amusedly pessimistic forecast. It was a seven of diamonds.

One of the patrons chortled.

"Be kind enough to put down a heart or a spade," Trevor added.

A six of clubs.

A five of diamonds.

Some patron asked, "Is there so little variety in this pack of cards?"

"I would call it singular if two ranks hadn't appeared," someone else returned.

"Not even a picture card has materialized."

"Myself, I always say that if I get a picture card within the first two minutes of a game, then I will emerge with a fatter purse. Occasionally it turns out to be the truth."

Belatedly the first man asked the others, "Can we all now be quiet in this room except for those at the table?"

No one pointed out that it was he who had opened the meeting for discussion. There couldn't have been a clearer indicator of everyone's tension.

A six of hearts was put down next.

Every witness knew with a thrill that one of the players must have been affected by this development. Royde's features showed nothing, except that his eyes seemed to have sharpened even further. He hadn't looked away from Trevor since the last time Camilla had glanced his way.

And at this time every patron's eyes seemed to follow Will Royde's. The Duke of Strafford suddenly shot to his feet.

"Damn!" he called out bitterly. "Damnation!"

Before anyone in the room could make another move, Trevor had ripped his own pasteboard in a burst of energy. He threw it onto the deck and raised that and took it several steps to the nearest window. There he parted the curtains, opened the panel, and hurled out the cards into the street below.

Royde had stood up, but not with nearly the quickness that Trevor showed. His complexion appeared to sport several shades of red in different places. Considering that he had emerged as victor, his response was in its own way as unseemly as Trevor's.

"Hearts!" Trevor said bitterly, and he must have been thinking of that special symbol as referring to love. "Damn all hearts!"

He started to the door.

Camilla called out, "You mustn't give up!"

Never would she have supposed herself capable of making any public display of emotion, but Trevor's previous outburst had proved infectious. Half a dozen steps took her in the Duke's direction before his hearing told him what was happening, and he turned back.

Now he spoke quietly so that it would have been difficult for anyone beyond Will Royde to hear.

"There is no further choice," he said. "I have lost."

"But—but you cannot let a game of cards determine what will happen to us," she insisted. Under this great agitation it seemed remarkable that she, too, could modulate her tones.

"I agreed to accept the results when I came to play and can do no other in all honesty."

Those last words appeared to vitalize Royde. He moved in Camilla's direction. Momentarily fearful that he would stand beside her, Camilla pulled away.

"So you think that all of us are quits, do you?" Royde asked in a tone that didn't make it sound like a question. Nor did he give the impression that he had determined upon some answer that agreed with the Duke's.

"How do you mean?" Trevor spoke softly to his former rival.

"You have just reacted powerfully when a card in a certain rank was put down on the side where any player who had previously been dealt that rank is the loser." Royde was choosing his words with the greatest care. "But the game itself has not yet been concluded."

"What more can you want? As I have decidedly lost, there is nothing else to be said."

"But *I* might have lost on the next deal." Royde was thin-lipped in anger. "The point at issue is that I have not officially won."

"My position, in turn, is that as far as I am involved, the game has been completed." Trevor was speaking sharply without raising his voice. "It was agreed that the matter in contention between us be settled by gaming and this has been done. I have lived up to the letter of our agreement, as everybody in this room except you will be only too pleased to testify."

"You have made it impossible to conclude the contest in a fashion which is universally recognized."

"A loss by one of the players should be conclusive anywhere on earth," Trevor insisted. "Should you feel differently, I invite you to employ another deck of cards and thereby reach a conclusion more satisfactory to you."

"I cannot do that now, in light of your vandalism, and still be called an honorable man as long as you decline to game any further on so fragile an excuse." Royde was white-faced now. "Of this, Your Grace, I am sure that you are very much aware."

Trevor appeared to consider the situation that had arisen.

"If I refuse to deny a defeat and you decline to accept a victory, then it seems to me that Miss—the lady in question—is a free agent, and that she may now choose whom she will in marriage. Isn't that so?"

Camilla laughed.

Royde was making a pair of fists as he turned, but unmade them in a moment. Clearly he was looking at a girl who followed the Duke's thoughts with pleasure, who relished the qualities of his darting intelligence and his presence as well. Camilla's admiration for the Duke and Strafford's glow in the light of it had become so plain that no witness could now mistake their feelings.

"Very well," Royde said in a different tone than Camilla had ever heard from him. "I have been defeated by these most clever tactics, Your Grace. I hereby release Miss Fairfield from —from my attentions. That should be satisfactory to you both."

Camilla found herself too stirred for the thanks she wanted to give, and not only to Royde.

"Three cheers and a tiger," Royde added bitterly. "Now I must do the polite thing, the good-mannered thing, as always. I must ask you to pardon me. I must ask you both to pardon me."

And without another word he whirled around towards the back gambling room in the direction of the staircase up to his office.

Camilla didn't expect Trevor to suddenly take her in his arms before so many people, but she hoped for some added recognition of her importance to him. Even a smile would have been sufficient at this time.

Instead, as she looked at him unbelievingly, he ducked his head in acknowledgment of a female's presence and nothing more. He spoke formally.

"It has been gratifying to have your assistance," said Trevor Drawhill, the Duke of Strafford.

Before Camilla could protest with so much as one word, he had turned away and was leaving the room.

CHAPTER TWENTY-THREE

"I changed my mind," Will Royde was saying pompously to Edith Jessop. "I have no further interest in the Fairfield chit, none at all."

They sat in his office, the door open at Royde's insistence. Edith had been requested by one of the waiters to go upstairs. Her heart hammered with anxiety to hear what he'd be saying, but she had made a point of walking up slowly to join him in this large room, with its Gothic Revival desk and gleaming chairs.

"It's no concern of mine now." Edith risked some belligerence to draw out his feelings swiftly.

"Oh, come on!" He tried to smile, although one palm was suddenly rubbing his overactive midriff. "I've been dismal a whole day and I think it's because you weren't around."

Royde was certain that his unhappiness had been exacerbated at sight of Camilla Fairfield reveling in Strafford's talk and the Duke preening in return. Royde had often preened when in Edith's company, taking such pleasure because she made him feel like the king of the largest hill in the world.

"You've been poorly because you didn't 'ave *me* cooking for you," Edith insisted, her sympathy awakened by seeing this particular man in distress.

Royde said stubbornly, "I hate to think of you being with me *and* soiling your hands in the kitchen betweentimes."

"But who else will cook *capons à l'escarlate* for you better than I will? Eh?"

"You might give the recipe to a cook."

"Don't think you can gammon me! A paid cook don't 'ave that personal concern for a man's tummy, Willie Royde! Would a cook care enough to make the tomato sauce just the way you like it for your filets of beef?"

Royde agreed silently, adding to himself that veal croquettes, another favorite, tasted best when Edith prepared them. His stomach had been prime, jibbing at nothing, when Edith had taken charge of it. And considering how well his carrottop, as he thought of her, looked now, dignified and demure as well as fetching, he wouldn't have to apologize to anyone that his wife was also a superb cook.

It was the first time he had thought seriously of Edith marrying him. The idea was far from unpleasant, but he knew it would show a lack of discretion to talk about it so quickly after this night's extraordinary happenings.

At the moment his strongest desire was to walk off with Edith on his arm and talk to her. Perhaps she would allow him a kiss. Possibly she would return it.

"Shall we take a stroll?" he asked softly. "The moon is very large, and the night looks pleasant."

Arthur Fairfield had spent the last minutes in a state of torpor relieved only by the knowledge that Camilla had at last been set free of Will Royde's attentions. He had been too distraught to offer Camilla the least help getting home, and now felt sure she wouldn't need his assistance in locating a four-wheeled growler on Bennet Street. The disappointment had been caused in the main by that deaf banker, Wolverstone, being unable to respond to Arthur's pleas and pretend Arthur was an employee. As a result Vivien bristled at his side and Vivien's aunt glowered behind her.

"If only you hadn't lied about being a useful worker," Vivien said for the fifteenth or sixteenth time.

"My coming here doesn't prove I lied," Arthur insisted weakly. "Camilla was so deeply involved I had to come."

"Then what is the name of that firm by which you are employed?" Vivien prodded. "Tell me that, Arthur Fairfield, then prove your honesty and trustworthiness, and I forgive you anything else."

He looked away awkwardly, not wanting to face her. The sight of Will Royde walking into this crowded room gave him an excuse to walk off with apologies, although he had nothing he wanted to say to one of the night's celebrities.

Royde turned in Arthur's direction, aware of owing the younger man a favor from earlier in the evening.

To justify a moment's talk Arthur said, "You ought to instruct your people to lay out tables and start a night's gaming. This is a large and wealthy group here."

"Yes. Yes, indeed." It pleased Royde that young Fairfield remained willing to be of genuine help after everything that had happened. "One moment and—and we will speak further."

He asked Edith to wait as well and busied himself giving appropriate orders. By the time Royde returned, Vivien and her aunt were in earshot yet again, having approached for further hope at a reconciliation and for added intense glowering, respectively.

"It occurs to me that you might be in the position to do me a favor and make out a little bit of all right as a result yourself," Royde said. He didn't choose to add that he was considering shortly mounting an excursion to Gretna Green with Edith, where they could be married quickly and without fuss. He preferred that sort of arrangement, but not nearly as much as he knew she would. After the ceremony a honeymoon trip to Hastings, in Sussex, the best of resorts, would be very pleasant. "I will soon need somebody to oversee my establishment for a few weeks."

"Me?" Arthur was astonished. "You'd want me to supervise the running of this place?"

"You're honest and bright, both," Royde remarked, opinions which elicited no dispute in this company. "Of course you'll have plenty of time to learn the workings and then you'll be able to make sure everybody does his job. Later I could pay for your services much more often and take a little time away every week to spend with my—well, that's no nevermind, right now! When I return from a brief walk with Miss Jessop you can give me your answer or leave it for me with one of the waiters."

He walked off again. Vivien, stunned though she was, managed to say, "A gambling hell! You would be an overseer in a gambling hell!"

Arthur winced at the prospect of Vivien's aunt also responding to this new stimulus. He had, however, underestimated the doughty Mrs. Malbot. Keenly aware of her recent dispute with an undoubtedly respectable banker, she was letting that recollection fuel her reaction to the prospect of her niece's husband making a career for himself as a factotum in a gambling mecca.

"I am inclined to feel that his work here would be more honest than that of most bankers," Mrs. Malbot said briskly and surprisingly. "A premium is put upon honesty here, unlike the ideology that prevails in banking hells—if I may speak of those for once with accuracy."

Arthur was no more taken aback by this *volte-face* than Vivien.

Mrs. Malbot spoke briskly to her niece. "And if he wishes to subsequently expend his intelligence and honesty in other fields, he will have already learned the pleasures and precepts of employment. I wholeheartedly approve such a career as a beginning at the least, and the forthcoming marriage as well."

"Aunt!" Vivien was joyful now.

"Indeed, I hope to eventually dandle the first grandniece or grandnephew on a knee. Also the second and third and fourth and fifth and sixth, *ad infinitum.*"

It was a dazed Arthur Fairfield who reached out a hand for Vivien, and an equally dazed Vivien who clasped it and returned an affectionate squeeze.

CHAPTER TWENTY-FOUR

Camilla returned to Lower Brook Street in a sullen mood. She had expected to spend time with Trevor following the game, and was dismayed that he had left Royde's place by himself.

"Will Royde has released me," she told Mamma and Sir Osric, who were ensconced in the small sitting room and waiting for her.

Lady Fairfield noticed her daughter's lack of joy. "Won't the Duke be offering for you?"

"I'm not sure what he will be doing."

Camilla sat quietly in her room until a series of urgent knocks came at the door. Lady Fairfield pattered in, her color higher with excitement.

"*He* is downstairs and I have put him in the large sitting room," she said without taking a breath. "Trevor, the Duke of Strafford! Oh, what a handsome son-in-law!"

Camilla wasn't certain that a wedding at St. George's in Hanover Square might be in the offing, but she felt considerably perked up by news of the visit. Briefly she inspected herself in the glass, touching a sprig of blond hair into place. Except for what she always imagined was a jutting chin, she liked what she saw.

In a corner of the glass she was able to see Lady Fairfield looking respectable in light blue. With difficulty she kept from smiling.

"You should wear a neckline lower off the shoulders," she said, grinning now as she criticized her mother's rig-out for the first time. She herself had so often been sternly rebuked from the same source.

The two women's eyes met. Lady Fairfield's younger daughter was plainly inferring that she, too, was now a member of the adult community. Lady Fairfield chuckled understandingly and nodded in full and happy agreement.

Camilla had instructed herself to walk slowly but, unlike Edith Jessop in a similar crisis, moved with the greatest celerity. She had further instructed herself to leave the door wide open, but closed it three quarters of the way as soon as she was inside the large sitting room.

Trevor's handsome features were slightly drawn by weariness. All the same, he saw the play of emotions on her face. He said swiftly, "I walked out of Royde's place without you, as I felt it could be hurtful to your reputation if I was alone with you afterwards."

She wondered if he was preparing her for the news that she was now totally free of his attentions as well as Royde's. The thought was chilling.

"Perhaps you didn't want it known that I might be sympathetic to someone whose behavior at a game of chance will be questioned everywhere, from the Adelphi to York Column."

"It might have been not only questioned but deplored—by me, if no one else, had I been forced to employ some of the tactics for which I had come prepared."

She still wasn't distracted from the major issue under advisement, but kept herself from directly asking the question that was most important to her.

"To what do you refer?" she asked instead, accommodating his wish.

"I had brought amenable dice with me in case a game of hazard was to be played for your future," Trevor informed her. "And some special cards, of course."

Now she felt watery-kneed, as he claimed to have cared so much about her future as to put his own into the discard with all society had he been caught.

"The cards?" she asked weakly.

"In different pockets of my clothing I carried ten white pasteboards of each rank," Trevor clarified. "I could have fumbled ostentatiously, pretending some indispositon, and pulled out the necessary card to give me a victory."

"But you didn't." Her face had fallen.

"We were playing faro at your insistence," he said gently, "and you had dealt me a card in the heart rank. I didn't believe that the results could possibly be adverse to me."

Her own heart was pounding faster. It moved her to know that Trevor had been immobilized by the nearness of a symbol for love, true love.

"When the worst did suddenly happen I acted on impulse and caused such a scene that the game couldn't be completed according to the rules. Part of my intelligence was aware that Royde, for the sake of his reputation, was unable to accept a tainted triumph."

Camilla swept that point aside with a gesture, not caring about Will Royde or his reputation.

"Fortunately, too, he saw the way your face looked when I was debating with him, and was aware that never could he bring forth such a reaction from you." Trevor considered. "So you see, Camilla, both of us caused Royde to abandon his scheme to marry you against your will."

She knew now that Trevor had adopted Royde's marital plan, with one significant change.

In a different tone he said, "I recognized you as Lady Fortune when we met for the second time at the May Ball, Camilla, but I felt you wanted that particular secret kept."

"Yes, I—I did, then." She was hardly able to speak.

"And I was ready to offer for you towards the end of your visit to my home in Kent, but that was the time when you chose to break off relations between us."

She remembered the occasion, to be sure. It had been impossible for her to guess that he was still not so agitated at the notion of so many females hunting for husbands, and that he himself had been brought down.

"Now," he said softly, "it is necessary for both our sakes to put away all masks. You are no longer a hoyden visitor to a gambling house, and I am no longer the elusive quarry wanting to camouflage himself by seeming to have been caught in marriage. I want to be actually caught."

"The masks are now put away," she agreed soberly.

"In that case, and with no further impediment over our features, we can establish a greater propinquity."

After those words he put both arms around Camilla's waist to bring her closer and lowered his lips to hers.

Lady Fairfield, who had briefly approached the sitting room door from the other side, closed it soundlessly and hurried upstairs.

"I believe that all is well at last," she told Sir Osric, who was taking his ease in the small sitting room.

The diplomat, true to form, responded, "I feel sure it is if you say so, my dear."

"I do indeed say so," Lady Fairfield beamed. "I do indeed."